"I'D LIKE TO SEE YOU AGAIN," TY SAID, GOING FOR broke.

"I'm sure we'll see each other, Mr. Garrett. Talbot is quite small and—"

"If it was the kiss, I could apologize."

Her crestfallen gaze flicked up to meet his.

"I wouldn't want to," he said quickly. "Apologize, that is, for kissing you. Not when it wasn't my fault. And I liked it too much for you to apologize to me."

"I beg your pardon?"

"I was more than ready to oblige when you asked me to kiss you," he explained.

"Mr. Garrett, let me assure you, I never asked you to kiss me or anybody else. Not one word of such a request ever—"

"You didn't say it out loud. But you were looking at my mouth, and the way you were looking made me think of kissing."

Her gaze inadvertently slipped down to his smile, and she remembered. His lips had been warm, his breath so soft blowing against her skin. "I—I can't be held responsible for your imagination."

"No doubt about it, Miss Willoughby," he drawled, leaning over her. "When you look at me like that, I get to thinking about kissing."

WHAT ARE *LOVESWEPT* ROMANCES?

They are stories of true romance and touching emotion. We believe those two very important ingredients are constants in our highly sensual and very believable stories in the LOVESWEPT line. Our goal is to give you, the reader, stories of consistently high quality that may sometimes make you laugh, sometimes make you cry, but are always fresh and creative and contain many delightful surprises within their pages.

Most romance fans read an enormous number of books. Those they truly love, they keep. Others may be traded with friends and soon forgotten. We hope that each LOVESWEPT romance will be a treasure—a "keeper." We will always try to publish

LOVE STORIES YOU'LL NEVER FORGET
BY AUTHORS YOU'LL ALWAYS REMEMBER

The Editors

Loveswept® 626

THE COURTING COWBOY

GLENNA
McREYNOLDS

BANTAM BOOKS
NEW YORK · TORONTO · LONDON · SYDNEY · AUCKLAND

THE COURTING COWBOY
A Bantam Book / July 1993

*If you would be interested in receiving protective vinyl covers for your
Loveswept books, please write to this address for information:*

Loveswept
Bantam Books
P.O. Box 985
Hicksville, NY 11802

ISBN 0-553-44355-0

Published simultaneously in the United States and Canada

*Bantam Books are published by Bantam Books, a division of Bantam Dou-
bleday Dell Publishing Group, Inc. Its trademark, consisting of the words
"Bantam Books" and the portrayal of a rooster, is Registered in U.S. Patent
and Trademark Office and in other countries. Marca Registrada. Bantam
Books, 1540 Broadway, New York, New York 10036.*

PRINTED IN THE UNITED STATES OF AMERICA.

OPM   0 9 8 7 6 5 4 3 2 1

For Anita—a cowboy, of course!

ONE

From where Ty Garrett stood on his back porch he could see everything he loved in the world and just about everything he hated. He hated drought, and there was plenty of drought to go around in northeastern Colorado. He hated to think he'd never be able to get ahead of himself financially, but one look at the ramshackle ranch buildings and the dust blowing with the cold autumn wind was enough to make him wonder if he would ever catch up with a decent living, let alone get ahead of one.

His gaze shifted, following the sheer cliffs rising out of the plains to the north, part of the boundary to his land. The chalk walls of the escarpment gleamed amber with the last reflected rays of the sunset, while a dark prairie sky pulled across the heavens from the east. Winter was getting ready to come on good, when there'd be snow piling up in the coulees, the land turning white to the horizon, long nights spent in front of the stove, and short days spent working hard to survive. He had no complaints about winter, but he hated to think he might spend the rest of his life without a woman to share the seasons with year after year, especially the nights. He'd been alone that way for a long time.

Amy Lambert had been making eyes at him again in church on Sunday, but Ty was sure another man's wife was the quickest road to ruin. She was sweet-looking, though, all blond hair and blue eyes, with pink blushes that got a man wondering what in the world she was thinking about.

Grinning wryly, he lowered his gaze and scuffed his boot across the boards of the porch. He knew what she was thinking about all right, but he wouldn't be messing himself up with Amy Lambert. A man had to draw lines he never crossed, no matter how long the nights.

He sighed and looked back to the house, through the window framing the kitchen and the young boy huddled over the schoolbooks lying open on the table.

Ty loved living on the grassland, roping calves, riding colts, and working the ranch. But there was nothing on God's green earth that made him feel love like the boy in the kitchen, Corey Allen Garrett. He'd made some mistakes in his life, and some had said keeping his son had been the biggest. Adoption, they said, was the only sensible solution for unwed teenagers. But Ty had never had regrets, not in twelve years.

"Dad!" Corey hollered without looking up from his books. "Come here, Dad. I'm stuck."

Ty groaned. When he'd left, Corey had been working on his science homework. The new teacher, Miss Willoughby, was a stickler for homework. So far he and Corey were barely keeping up, and Parents' Night was Thursday. He didn't want Corey to get behind when he had to go in and face the teacher himself. Especially when he would already have one strike against him by being late because of a construction job he'd picked up on the side.

"Dad!" Corey yelled again.

Ty pushed off the porch rail, grinning at his own cowardice. One little old widow lady from back east couldn't be too hard to handle, despite what he'd heard about her strange ways and fancy degrees. He just wished that once every blue moon or so a good-looking, not so old, eligible marrying kind of woman would show up within a fifty-mile radius of Talbot, Colorado.

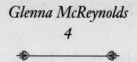

Victoria Miranda Elizabeth Willoughby cleared her throat unsuccessfully twice before reaching for the water glass on her desk. She thought things were going rather well for her first Parents' Night. Her dearly departed husband, Charles Edward Willoughby IV, certainly hadn't educated her

to end up teaching the children of farmers and ranchers in the vast emptiness of the American West. Still, she hadn't lived with a peer of the British realm without learning how to stiffen her backbone and call upon her reserves. *Chin up, Victoria*, had been the rallying cry of her youth, and marrying her mentor had changed little except their sleeping arrangements.

"As I was saying," she continued after taking a sip of water. "My goal is to have the seventh- and eighth-graders firmly grounded in the scientific method before we break for the Christmas holidays. The requirements for the high school students will, of course, be—"

The classroom door squeaked open, interrupting her and drawing everyone's attention. Victoria frowned. She usually gave demerits for tardiness, but demerits hardly seemed appropriate for Parents' Night. Then again, the man coming in late hardly seemed old enough to be the parent of one of her teenage students.

He closed the door behind him and gave her a short nod, touching the brim of a gray sweat-stained cowboy hat.

"Ma'am," he said, and a slow, easy smile broke across his face.

Victoria's heart fluttered.

She quickly cleared her throat again and returned the greeting with a prim glance. She didn't know what else to do. It was quite beyond her how women coped with the average western American male, especially the ones called cowboys. They were so unlike the men she'd always known, so unlike her husband and her father.

She finished her sentence and moved on to her philosophy of teaching. But out of the corner of her eye she noticed the man wasn't moving away from the door. She took a calming breath and returned her attention to him.

"There are a few empty desks toward the back," she said, asserting her authority.

His smile broadened, creasing his sun-browned cheeks and revealing strong white teeth. Her heart fluttered again.

"I didn't fit in a desk when I was supposed to," he said. "I don't think there's much hope for it now."

The other parents chuckled, and her gaze inadvertently slid down the rugged length of his body, across a broad chest, narrow hips, and long legs. Her cheeks flushed. "Well, yes, hmm, I see the problem. There's a chair in my library corner. You're welcome to use it."

"Thank you, ma'am." He gave her another smile, and she experienced another distressful reaction in her chest.

"You're—you're welcome," she stammered, wondering what in the world was coming over her.

She continued on with her speech, calming herself with the carefully rehearsed words. A minute later, though, her gaze strayed to the man making his way to the back of her classroom. He was particularly unlike the men she'd grown up with, she thought with exasperation as she watched him step over a desk to shake someone's hand and draw more attention to himself. When he leaned even farther over to greet another man, her eyes widened despite herself. He was straddling the desk in a position that did shocking things to his otherwise properly fitting jeans. Her breath stopped for a moment, until he finished his social business and moved on toward the chair in the back. Really, she wondered, still aghast, what did a woman do with a man like that?

The cowboy found the chair and sat down, taking off his hat and giving her his attention. She momentarily repaid him in kind, just to make sure he stayed put. Her quick glance took in the rich brown color of his hair and the liveliness of his light gray eyes.

He was attractive, she supposed, in a fresh, outdoorsy way. His features were well made and even, a genetic blessing that had nothing to do with a person's character—she'd learned that from an unfortunate personal experience—but the cowboy was handsome nonetheless. She liked the way the dark slashes of his eyebrows contrasted with the pale color of his eyes. It was intriguing, safely so, not like the business with his legs and his muscles and his jeans. He radiated energy and life, a distinct difference from Charles, who had been quite infirm his last few years.

She went back to her speech, wishing the parents would show more enthusiasm and interest. So far they were about as animated as her seventh-period class, the highlight of the evening apparently having been the latecomer. She checked him again after a few minutes, for no special reason, and was surprised to find him yawning.

So much for her radiant-energy-of-youth theory, she thought with another twinge of exasperation. She raised her voice a degree, relying on a time-proven lecture strategy to rekindle everyone's interest.

Ty stifled another yawn, thinking Corey had been right. Miss Willoughby did look like an owl, a baby owl with its feathers all stuck out. "Like one of those burrowing owlets we found in the south pasture last spring," he'd said. "Remember how cute they were, drying out after the rain?"

It was her glasses, Ty decided. They were so perfectly round, and she blinked in slow motion as if she were very tired. Every time her glasses slid down her too-small nose, it took her longer and longer to push them back up. She would give the classroom full of parents a slow, inquiring look over the tortoiseshell rims, expecting questions that she seldom got, then with a near-imperceptible sigh push her glasses up and continue with her speech.

The wet-feathers part was a bit more of an exaggeration, but Ty understood where his son had gotten the impression. Her hair was naturally curly to an untameable degree, her one hundred and one misplaced bobby pins notwithstanding. The color was mostly brown, but there were a few auburn strands woven through the brownness. He couldn't say the same for her outfit. Her sweater was plain dark brown and reached past her hips, covering half of her plain brown skirt, but he thought he detected some nice feminine curves under all the brownness. Past her skirt, her stockinged legs were pale, and she wore a pair of sturdy plain brown shoes.

She did look like an owl, a slightly lost, somewhat overwhelmed baby owl. The resemblance was remarkable, except he'd never seen legs as pretty as hers on any bird. Her knees were fine-boned, and without having to lean too far over in his chair, he could see her ankles.

Tilting his head to one side, he leaned the extra inch necessary. Her ankles were also nice, very nice. He'd always thought women's ankles were sexy, and Miss Willoughby definitely had some of the best he'd seen. Not that great ankles alone meant anything, or that he meant anything by admiring them. She really didn't look to be his type. Lacey Kidder, his seventy-year-old neighbor, didn't think he was putting enough effort into finding out just exactly what kind of woman was his type. And if he didn't, she said, by golly, she was going to start. It was time he was married, she said. Past time, actually.

He'd have to tell Lacey he'd figured out one thing: The right woman couldn't go wrong if she had ankles like Miss Willoughby. He leaned a little farther to the left—and fell off his chair.

He barely caught himself, and he made a lot of noise doing it, planting his boot hard on the floor and scraping the chair. When it was all over, he looked up and found Miss Willoughby staring at him.

"Are you quite comfortable now?" she asked with a civilized amount of condemnation in her voice, the dark, delicate wings of her eyebrows rising above her tortoiseshell rims.

She could have ignored the incident, but she'd chosen confrontation instead. Coming from the diminutive Miss Willoughby, he liked the choice. When she continued to give him one of *those* looks, he started to laugh. He'd have to add "spirited" to Lacey's list.

"Quite comfortable, now. Thank you, ma'am."

She blushed, and he realized she was a lot easier to embarrass than he was. Her tough exterior went about as deep as prairie topsoil. Surprisingly, he found himself liking that too.

"I believe," Miss Willoughby continued, her cheeks a faint shade of pink, "that an academic trinity of parent, child, and teacher creates the optimum learning environment. A great deal of my own education was attained in this manner, literally in the field at my father's knee. I was also quite fortunate to have continued my studies under the guidance of his esteemed colleague, Charles

Willoughby . . . Charles Edward Willoughby the Fourth."

She repeated the name after a short pause, as if she expected the people in the room to recognize it, but Ty figured she was shooting in the dark. For the most part, the folks around Talbot didn't keep up with the goings-on of the Royal Geographic Society and the Explorers Club, groups she mentioned at every opportunity. He was beginning to understand why people thought she was snooty, and why the school board thought she was such a catch. He was having a harder time figuring out why Corey liked her so much. His son had never worked harder for a teacher. He and Ty did science assignments even on the rare night when she didn't assign anything. Ty thought his son was a little young to be an ankle man, and as far as he could tell, she was drier than toast. But she wasn't as old as he'd expected.

And she did have something about her, a kind of innocent, painstaking seriousness that made a person feel as though she were telling them the God's truth with every word she spoke. It was interesting, and maybe a little disconcerting.

"Mr. Willoughby and I," she was continuing, "eventually married, and together founded the Willoughby Institute of Natural History Research and Education."

In fact, she wasn't nearly as old as he'd expected, and she had a nice voice, very soothing and feminine. Given the lack of female companionship in their lives, her voice might be one of the main reasons Corey liked her. She didn't speak like anyone else they knew. She had an accent. It wasn't French, or southern, or British, or anything else Ty could put his finger on, but it was cultured.

Hiding another yawn, he checked his watch and stretched his legs out into the aisle. He had already decided to skip the rest of Parents' Night. He'd heard Ann Riverson's English speech three years running, and Glen Frazer, the principal, always wound up the evening by wheedling favors.

Ty was favored out. He stretched his legs again and ran his hand over his eyes. He was so damn tired. He should be asleep in bed, not sitting in a schoolroom, listening to Miss Willoughby's sweet, uppity voice tell him all about the merits of earth science, natural history, and her dead husband's institute.

Victoria frowned at the cowboy nodding drowsily in the corner of her classroom. Surely he wasn't going to fall asleep in her library corner, not in the middle of her presentation. He'd been fighting the inclination for the last quarter hour. Couldn't he hold on for another few minutes?

She did a quick visual check of the other people in the room. There weren't any signs of rapt fascination, but no one else was falling asleep. She looked back at the exhausted rabble-rouser, ready to reproach him with a steely glare, but she was too late.

Her lips tightened, and the barest blush of indignation colored her cheeks. The cowboy had fallen asleep. She could tell by the soft snores emanating from her library corner and by the quiet chuckles of his nearest neighbors. As more people noticed, the tittering increased until every person in the room had taken a moment to crane his neck to see what was going on.

Victoria did not take this final insult in stride. He was making a mockery of her teaching skills, and in front of the very people she needed to impress. They would no doubt all go home and wonder if their children were sleeping through her lectures too.

With her chin up she forged ahead, ignoring him as best she could. A lady in the middle of the room raised her hand, and Victoria gratefully gave the woman her undivided attention and a thorough answer to her question.

Maybe too thorough, she thought when no

other hands went up. Resigned, she concluded her speech, and people immediately started getting up and leaving. Her husband had often lectured her on the importance of thoroughness when speaking, but he'd also insisted on the speaker not taking liberties with the audience's time. One should never bore, Charles had always said.

Her gaze slid again to the cowboy in the corner. She took in the relaxed slump of his broad shoulders beneath his worn plaid shirt and the lazy sprawl of his legs stretched out into the aisle. Dust caked his soft jeans and his boots, none of it stirred by so much as a twitch. His gray hat, worn and creased from years of wear, dangled from the fingers of one large, rough hand. Truth be told, he looked like she'd bored him to death.

She turned and set her lecture notes on her desk, and a small, irritated sigh escaped her. No one had ever fallen asleep during one of Charles's presentations. They wouldn't have dared.

She cast another glance at the man in the corner and was relieved to see one of his neighbors stop and give him a shake. Thank goodness she'd been saved the humiliation of having to wake him. She'd surely done enough by putting him to sleep in the first place.

"Miss Willoughby," a familiar voice called behind her. "Oh, Miss Willoughby."

Stifling another sigh, Victoria turned, a half-hearted smile on her face, to see the school principal bustling into her classroom. Mr. Frazer was bald and portly, cheerful and kind, and usually in need of a favor. She was too tired to grant favors this evening. Teaching children was the most exhausting thing she'd ever done in her whole life.

"Mr. Frazer." She greeted him with polite formality, her smile holding steady. "How kind of you to stop by."

"Nothing kind about it at all, Miss Willoughby. I wanted to check on— Ah, there he is." Mr. Frazer waved at someone behind her. "Ty, come on over here."

Victoria glanced over her shoulder, and her smile faded. Her pulse picked up in speed. Whatever Mr. Frazer wanted, she preferred not to be involved if it included that man. He'd caused one scene by arriving late and two more by falling out of his chair and falling asleep, and she didn't even want to think about the start he'd given her heart when he'd straddled the desk. Given his age, she was sure there wasn't any reason for her to officially recognize him. They couldn't have a student in common.

"Excuse me," she said. "I think I'll—"

"Ty, good to see you," Mr. Frazer interrupted, pulling the younger man into the conversation while he was still a few steps behind her. Victoria attempted another escape, but Mr. Frazer effectively trapped her with his next words. "I wanted to make sure you met our Miss Willoughby."

"My pleasure, ma'am," the cowboy said, coming to a stop in front of her and extending his hand.

Forced by convention, Victoria returned the courtesy and found her palm and fingers engulfed in a warm, firm handshake. She glanced up and was startled to find him smiling down at her as if nothing had happened, as if he hadn't embarrassed her in front of the whole town. She was even more startled to realize his smile was generating as much heat as his hand, and that her heart was fluttering again. His teeth were very white against his darkly tanned face, giving his mouth a clean and inviting look. And that was the most startling thought of all.

Mr. Frazer finished the introductions. "And this is Ty Garrett, Corey's father."

"How do you do," Victoria managed to say in spite of her surprise at the information and at herself. Inviting mouth, indeed. Whatever did she mean by such a thought? As to Mr. Frazer's news, the only thing she could think was that Mr. Garrett must have married very young, and that Corey must resemble his missing mother. She knew the boy and his father lived alone, but no one had filled her in on the details.

She also thought Ty Garrett's eyes were even more intriguing up close, a most unusual color, a soft, clear gray of the rarest purity, and she was surprised to realize the observation wasn't purely academic. The exhaustion of long hours and long days must finally be taking a toll on her emotions, she decided.

"I'm doing better after my nap," he said in answer to her polite greeting. A definite, teasing light brightened the depths of his eyes.

She pulled her hand free, suddenly piqued, and told herself gray eyes weren't the least bit unusual. She didn't know what had come over her. The man was too rude, too irreverent, and too rough-edged for her tastes.

"I'm sure Corey is looking forward to the dance tomorrow night," Mr. Frazer said. "All the kids are, though most of the boys won't admit it."

"The children do seem excited," Victoria agreed, doing her best to hold up her end of the pointless conversation. Ty Garrett was also much too young for her tastes, she reminded herself. She liked mature men who had made a place for themselves in the world. Inviting mouth, indeed. What unadulterated silliness.

"We have had a small problem crop up with

the chaperones," Mr. Frazer continued. "Bob and Jessie Claypool were scheduled to chaperone, but his mom has come down sick, and they went to Denver last night. I was hoping I could count on you two to pick up the slack."

Not that she was looking for a man, for goodness sake. Poor Charles was barely cold in his grave, gone just two years.

"Miss Willoughby?"

She had continued with his work and would do so again as soon as she was over her current financial predicament. She certainly didn't need a man to guide her any longer. She'd had quite enough of guiding.

"Miss Willoughby?"

"Yes?" she replied with a start, realizing she'd been staring at the plaid pattern in Ty Garrett's shirt. Cowboy shirts were tapered and yoked, made to closely fit a man's body, a fact she'd been noticing in another surprisingly nonacademic manner.

"Great. I knew I could count on you." Mr. Frazer reached for her hand and pumped it up and down a few times as he turned his attention to Ty. "Ty, I hope you won't let me down. This little lady is going to need an escort, and you're about the only bachelor left, except for Harper, and I wouldn't let my oldest dog go out with Harper, or Lord forbid, get in that truck of his."

Victoria was embarrassed, and she was sure she should be offended, but things were moving a little quickly. She wasn't at all clear on what she'd agreed to do, or what Harper's truck and Mr. Frazer's old dog had to do with her.

Ty knew, and he could have kicked himself for getting so easily taken in by Glen Frazer. The man was wily, and he'd put Ty in a most awkward position.

He slanted a glance down at the "little old widow lady from back east." She still looked over-whelmed, lost, and tired, but she wasn't nearly old enough not to get her feelings hurt. Women never were.

She'd agreed to Glen's request, and Ty had been brought up to be God-fearing, honorable, and polite to women. He'd been thinking of head-ing over to Ault or Fort Collins for a few drinks and a good time tomorrow night, but going to the dance wouldn't be so awful, not even with the owlish Miss Willoughby. He'd certainly suffered through worse Friday nights, and he was sure he'd had worse dates.

He gave her another quick glance. Well, he was pretty sure anyway. He hoped she didn't talk about her dead husband all night.

"Glad to help out, Glen." He shook the other man's hand and turned to his son's science teacher.

"Miss Willoughby, I'll pick you up about five-thirty, if that's okay. The dances always start at six, and that'll give us enough time to make sure the sound system is set up."

She gave him a blank look, which pretty much mirrored his own level of enthusiasm, regardless of her nice ankles. Chaperoning a bunch of junior high school kids didn't make for many opportunities to admire a woman's legs.

"It's been real nice meeting you, ma'am," he added, and touched the brim of his hat, making his getaway before the principal came up with any more ideas.

Victoria was stunned. Mr. Frazer shook her hand one more time, but she barely noticed. She had a date. It was the most ridiculous thing that had ever happened to her. She'd never had a date in her life. Charles had taken her out to dinner the night he'd proposed, but the occasion had hardly seemed like a date. They'd been eating dinner together since her childhood, and after her father had died, it had usually been just the two of them anyway.

But this was different. She had a date with a male of the subspecies *Western americanus cowboyius*, and she wasn't at all sure she was up to it.

TWO

"Ridiculous," Victoria muttered, hanging up the phone for the hundredth time. Ty Garrett's phone number had been reduced to a smear of ink on the paper clutched in her hand, but that was the least of her problems. She'd memorized his phone number hours before.

She glanced down at her dress, a blousy silk thing she'd never been sure looked right on her. The dress had been expensive—all of her clothes were—but this particular piece of her wardrobe was flouncy and bouncy, not at all her usual more tailored style. The colors seemed all right, white with orange poppies outlined in black, and a beige trellis pattern splashed willy-nilly in the background. She still kept getting the feeling the dress would look better on someone taller.

She needed to call Mr. Garrett and make a

polite excuse for that night. He could probably handle forty-three junior high school students with one arm tied behind his back. He didn't need her help. He probably didn't want her help. She was sure he wasn't looking forward to her company any more than she was looking forward to his. They didn't even know each other. What in the world had Mr. Frazer been thinking to pair them as chaperones? It must be obvious to even the most untrained eye that they had absolutely nothing in common.

Was the dress as awful as she feared, or was it just her nerves making it look lopsided?

She had to call Mr. Garrett. That's all there was to it. She had to call Mr. Garrett before he showed up on her doorstep. She refused to feel guilty about going back on her word. She hadn't even known what she was agreeing to do. Or was it that she hadn't actually agreed to do anything and Mr. Frazer had taken undue advantage of a moment's confusion?

That was it. She was positive.

She gripped the telephone receiver with renewed determination, and it rang in her hand. She sucked in her breath and stepped back. The phone rang again. It had to be him, Mr. Garrett.

What was happening to her life? she wondered in dismay. Everything had always been so safe and predictable. Men had never called her before, not strange men with teasing eyes and inviting smiles, not men who were so unsettling, so unknown, so—so unabashedly masculine.

She pulled the receiver off its hook and held it to her ear, answering the call before she worried herself out of her last ounce of courage, or her last ounce of sense. She wasn't sure which.

"Miss Willoughby?"

It *was* him. The lazy drawl and timbre of his voice were unmistakable.

"Speaking," she said, enunciating both syllables despite the breathlessness she felt.

"This is Ty Garrett. I'm real sorry, ma'am, but I'm going to be late picking you up."

"Oh." The small word was more a breath than a comment.

He went on to explain about a cow, and a fence, and what can happen when the two get all tangled up in each other. His voice was nicer than she remembered, older sounding, deep and soft like the pull of a slow-moving river, but without the soothing effect. Her heart was pounding so hard, she could barely decipher his story.

"Goodness," she said in an appropriate place, more by instinct than design, and sometime later she managed to add, "Certainly, I understand."

It was only after he'd hung up that she realized

she'd forgotten to mention she wouldn't be able to make it to the dance. Still holding on to the phone, she looked once more at her dress. Was it really as bad as she thought?

Ty was no fashion expert. The most he usually noticed about women's clothes was whether or not they highlighted something particularly intriguing underneath.

Standing on Miss Willoughby's front porch, he realized there was no way to tell with her dress. It was the ugliest thing he'd ever seen on a woman, bar none, and there was a lot of it, yards of orange splotches, beige grids, and black squiggles. Somebody should be shot for making such a dress and then hanged for selling it to Miss Willoughby.

"Evening, ma'am."

"Hello, Mr. Garrett." She stood in the doorway, her eyes wide and innocent behind her glasses, her voice polite and uppity, and her dress looking like something the cat had dragged in. He was having a hard time figuring her out.

"Since we're running late and all, I thought we should get right over to the school," he said, holding his hat in his hands and trying to keep from staring at her dress. "I had Corey wait in the truck."

"Of course."

"Let me help you," he said when she reached for her coat, a sturdy brown thing that looked as if it would outlive both of them. He wondered if she had anything pretty in her closet, or if everything she owned was either oversize, ugly, or brown.

He put his hat back on, then held her coat for her, thinking the night hadn't gotten off to a very good start. He was certainly feeling his share of awkwardness, and if the stiffness of her body was any indication, she wasn't comfortable with him either. Glen Frazer was going to owe both of them for this night's work.

When she was ready, he slipped the coat up her arms. Ugly dress, big brown coat, and all, she'd probably been a comfort to her husband, even a pleasure. No man could live with a woman and not notice how the light caught in her hair like the lamplight was catching in Miss Willoughby's. Her hair had a lot more auburn in it than he'd realized, giving her wild curls an overall chestnut color, not brown. She had pretty skin, too, more like cream than peaches, except for the faint color blooming on her cheeks.

The surprising evidence of emotion stymied him for a moment. Was he doing something to make her blush? He checked his hands and his distance and found both acceptable, much more acceptable than the thought that followed: Miss Willoughby's cream-colored skin being caressed by his own dark hands. The idea came out of nowhere, visually erotic and full-blown, and then it wouldn't go away.

He was privately embarrassed and a whole lot surprised. Lord, if he needed any further proof that he'd been too long without a woman, he sure didn't know what it would be. All it took was getting close enough to one to put on her coat, and he got to thinking in the craziest directions.

But Miss Willoughby did have pretty skin. Another look sent the fact home without a doubt. From her brow to her cheek to her chin, from the slope of her small nose to the slender column of her neck, she looked creamy-soft and silky, every square inch of her. He liked the way her upswept hairstyle and ineffective bobby pins left a few chestnut curls falling across her nape, but if he remembered correctly, it used to take more than the glimpse of a woman's neck to turn him on.

In his own defense, he added the fact that she smelled good, not like flowers and nothing as sensual as musk, but like sunshine-warmed woman, and he liked the scent. He liked it a lot. He was beginning to wonder just how tired he'd been the previous night. He seemed to have missed quite a bit when it came to the new science teacher. Of course, he hadn't been this close to her on Parents' Night. A good thing too, considering the effect she had on him when they did get close. He wondered if she knew it was Talbot tradition for the chaperones to dance the first dance together.

"Oh!" Her sharp gasp brought his wonderings to an abrupt halt.

"Excuse me," he muttered, feeling his own blush heating up to match hers. While slipping her coat over her shoulders, he'd somehow snagged the sleeve button on his suit jacket in one of her curls. He tried to untangle her hair by winding it one way, then the other. Both attempts made the situation worse.

"Oh!" she gasped again.

"Excuse me."

"Ouch!"

"I'm really sorry, ma'am." He felt like a total fool, and he was hurting her. Of the two, the last was the worst. "Maybe if I take my jacket off, I can get you free."

"Please do try, Mr. Garrett."

He did try, but found he couldn't get out of his jacket without her help.

"Would you pull on my other sleeve, please? I'll try not to let the button pull your hair anymore."

"Certainly," she replied, sounding breathlessly hopeful, which only made him feel worse.

Keeping the tangled sleeve close to her neck, he stepped around her so she'd have better access to his other sleeve. The result of all his maneuvering and her helping was to have them practically wrapped in each other's arms. The fact was lost on neither of them.

"Oh, my." Miss Willoughby breathed the words in near silence.

"We should have it in a minute," Ty promised, noticing how nicely she would fit against him if they got a little closer. "If you could just hold your sleeve tight while I try to get my elbow . . ."

"My sleeve?"

"I mean my sleeve."

"Of course."

"Yeah, like that. I'll just—" Lord, she had pretty skin, and her lips were full and looked soft and sweet.

Victoria didn't care what he was just about to do, but if he didn't do it quickly, she might faint. She was surrounded by him, and he was surprisingly warm, amazingly warm. Why, a woman could . . . Well, she didn't know what, but it was bound to be scandalous, what a woman did with a man like Ty Garrett.

"Mr. Garrett," she said, not liking the flustered tremble in her voice but unable to rectify the situation. She needed to assert herself, and a flimsy command was better than none.

"Yes?"

"Please hurry."

Ty didn't mistake her meaning for a minute. He didn't have a lot of experience with women, but he knew something was happening between them, something physically charged, and it wasn't all him. Her blush had spread like a soft pink mask across her face. Her eyes were mostly downcast, but they had flicked up more than once to meet his for an instant, and she'd wet her lips twice. Both times Ty had found himself moving closer to her. He'd swear she'd done the same. He'd almost given up on trying to shrug out of his jacket. It would be so easy to draw her near and kiss her.

But they were standing in her open doorway, and Corey was in the truck, and it wasn't as if they were having a real date, where mutual attraction had been established. Chaperoning a dance was more like public service than a romantic interlude. He was beginning to get ideas, though. Lots of ideas.

Victoria had some ideas of her own, ideas reminiscent of her previous, unmentionable indiscretion, but without the safety net of a husband who could save her from herself this time. Last night she hadn't been able to imagine what a woman did with a man like Ty Garrett, and now her imagination was running amok. He was so close, so broad in the shoulders. Her whole line of vision was taken up by his chest and the way the muscles moved in his arms; by the squared line of his jaw and the smooth, taut texture of his skin. She had to clench her free hand into a fist to keep from reaching up and touching him.

"Mr. Garrett, please," she pleaded.

Please what? Ty wondered. Mr. Garrett, please kiss me? Mr. Garrett, please take me in your arms? Or Mr. Garrett, please get your sleeve button out of my hair?

Ty played it safe and reasonable. He finished pulling his arm out of his coat, then slipped it off his other shoulder.

"Why don't you hold this while I try to get the button out of your hair?" he said, handing his coat to her.

She crushed the black jacket to her breasts. Ty let himself notice for a moment before forcing himself to concentrate on the job at hand—which wasn't the curves of white and orange material outlined against the dark cloth of his jacket.

As carefully as possible he started working her hair free, but it didn't take him more than a few seconds to realize there was nothing safe or reasonable about the task. He was bent over her neck, and she was overwhelming him with her scent, the softness of her skin against his fingers, and the feel of her hair in his hands.

She started to tremble, and he had a powerful urge to kiss her lips, to invade her mouth with his tongue, and slide his hands down her back and over her hips.

"What's your name?" he asked instead, but only after clearing his throat to make sure the words came out sounding normal.

"My name?" Startled brown eyes met his, but they weren't plain brown, he noticed. Her eyes were soft with rims of gold and moss-green sparks.

"Yes, your name," he said patiently, and tried to smile. "I was thinking maybe we could get beyond the Mr. Garrett–Miss Willoughby stage."

"Oh, I see. Yes. Victoria Miranda Elizabeth Willoughby." She recited it from top to bottom, like a child pulled in front of a schoolmaster.

"Victoria." He tried the name out. "That's real pretty."

Their eyes met over her shoulder.

"My name is Ty."

"I remember."

He nodded slowly, and his gaze drifted down

to her mouth. Her lips parted. Ty took a deep breath.

"I like Miranda too," he said.

"It's a moon in the Milky Way."

He wanted to kiss her. He wanted to kiss her so badly, he didn't dare do it.

"Mr. Garrett?" she said, her voice so soft he wouldn't have heard her if he'd been any farther away.

"Call me Ty, please."

"Ty," she agreed, her lashes lowering. A new infusion of color pinkened her cheeks. "I think my hair is free now. Thank you."

Ty looked at his hands. Strands of her silky hair were draped across his fingers where he'd been playing with it. The sleeve of his jacket had slipped over her shoulder and was lying against her bosom.

"Maybe we should get going," she suggested, offering him his jacket.

"Yeah. Maybe we should." Five more minutes of putting on Miss Victoria Willoughby's coat and he wouldn't be in any shape to chaperone anybody.

When they stepped off the porch, Corey jumped out of the truck and held the door open. He had a big smile for his science teacher, but

when she turned to climb into the pickup, he gave his dad a pointed, questioning look.

Ty lifted his eyebrows and shrugged. He was as surprised as his son by what had happened in her doorway. He hadn't planned to get tangled up in her hair or to get close enough to get in trouble, even imaginary trouble. The real surprise, though, waited for him at the dance.

Corey held him back at the doors to the gym, letting Miss Willoughby go on alone to relieve Glen Frazer. Ty looked down at his son and the small, strong hand the boy was resting on his sleeve. Though Corey's golden hair and the shape of his mouth were purely maternal, the gray eyes looking up at him and the boy's straight dark eyebrows were a perfect match for his own.

"What's up?" he asked.

"Dad, I know you don't get out much," Corey began, his gaze shifting from his dad's face to the floor. "But you've got it all backward. You're not supposed to kiss them at first."

"Them?" Ty asked after a moment of uncomfortable silence.

"Women," Corey explained, glancing up and giving his dad a little grin. "I just thought you should know you're doing it wrong."

Had he been that obvious? Ty wondered. And how could he have been doing anything wrong when he'd been trying hard not to do anything at all? And since when did his son know anything about kissing women?

"You're supposed to wait until the end of the date," Corey continued, "until you take them home, and that's only if they give you a signal."

"A signal?"

"Yeah, a signal." His son went on to enlighten him. "Lacey says it's kind of tricky, the signal. She says it takes a lot of experience to know when you're getting one, and well, you *don't* get out much, Dad. I don't think you gave Miss Willoughby enough time to give you a signal."

"Oh." Ty knew it had been a long while since he'd had a date, or anything resembling a date. He had a son to care for and a ranch to run. But he still thought he was in a better position to know about "signals" than a twelve-year-old boy who got his information secondhand from a seventy-year-old woman who hadn't had a date since the Great Depression.

"Maybe if you dance with her a couple of times and don't step on her or anything, she'll give you a signal," Corey suggested. "It's worth a try. She's awful pretty."

Ty glanced down at his son. "I thought you said she looked like an owl."

"Owls are pretty, Dad." It was an irrefutable statement of fact.

"Yeah, well, I don't think Miss Willoughby will be giving out any signals that we need to be worrying about," he said, hoping to put an end to the discussion.

The worried look coming over his son's face made him doubt his success. He could see Corey was thinking, and thinking hard, taking the whole situation more seriously than Ty would have thought possible.

"Maybe if you get her some punch when she's thirsty and don't spill it on her," Corey said, his face brightening. "And if you're real nice, and if you talk to her about science and stuff. She really likes science and you know all about it from helping with my homework." He stopped the flood of words and gave Ty a hopeful look. "You're real nice, Dad. I know she'd like you if you'd just help her along a little bit."

And having Miss Willoughby like him, it seemed, was very important to his son. Ty couldn't have been more surprised if the roof had fallen in.

"Just think about it, Dad, and if you need some more advice, we could call Lacey." With that Corey left to go find his friends.

"Uh, thanks." Ty didn't think he needed Lacey's advice, and he was a little annoyed that

Corey thought he did. He couldn't be that out-dated, could he?

He searched the dance floor until his gaze fell upon the science teacher with the pretty skin and kissable mouth. She was standing next to the refreshment table. Glen Frazer was shaking her hand and getting ready to leave. The kids were milling around the snacks, the boys pushing and pounding each other the way they always did, and the girls huddling and holding on to each other the way they always did.

Her dress was awful, even from a distance, but he remembered the gold and green in her eyes, and how her hair had felt silky and soft in his hands. He remembered the shy blush on her cheeks and the way she'd trembled when his fingers had brushed against her neck. Those were signals, all right, powerful signals guaranteed to get a man's attention. But what did Corey see when he looked at Victoria Willoughby?

More than a science teacher, that much was obvious. Maybe another friend like Lacey, except younger. Maybe a sort of scholastic mentor.

No, he decided. Corey was only twelve years old, a little young to be worrying about college.

Maybe a mother.

He let out a heavy breath and shoved his hands

into his pockets. It was natural for the boy to want a mother. But Miss Willoughby?

She turned then and caught him staring. Her hand went to her throat and her eyes widened behind her big, round glasses. Ty didn't back off. He kept looking, wondering if it was all men or just him who unnerved her so easily.

Suddenly he hoped it was just him, because she had completely unnerved him back at her house. Truth be told, he'd very much like her to do it again.

THREE

Victoria returned her attention to Mr. Frazer, but she knew Ty Garrett was still looking at her. She felt the heat of his gaze warming the back of her neck. The man was unbelievably effective at unsettling her. She'd hardly had a calm breath since he'd called. But they were at the dance now, and they both had duties that should preclude any more intimate encounters.

Intimate. The word crossed her mind, and her face flushed. She was being ridiculous. Having a button tangled up in one's hair was not an intimate encounter. Kissing and . . . other things were intimate, but not buttons.

Kissing. The color rose higher in her cheeks. He'd almost kissed her. Goodness knows why. She'd never been one to inspire impromptu kissing. Charles hadn't cared for it much, impromptu or otherwise. The only other occasion in her life when she'd been kissed had to do with her unmentionable indiscretion. Charles, of course, had mentioned it at length for a month of Sundays until he'd been quite sure she'd gotten such foolishness out of her system. She had, luckily so, because there was no one left to lecture her, no father, no husband. She was on her own with Ty Garrett—another disturbing thought.

"Victoria?"

She jumped at the sound of his voice and whirled around.

"Mr. Garrett?" she managed to answer.

"Ty," he reminded her.

"Of course. Ty." She wondered how a man could be so circumspect, so nice and friendly, and so damnably upsetting at the same time.

"The first dance is starting, and it's customary for the chaperones to lead off," he said, smiling down at her.

"Oh?" Victoria thought maybe she needed some fresh air. She retrieved a tissue from her dress pocket, then didn't know what to do with it. A warm, dry tissue wasn't going to save her. Embarrassed, she shoved it back into her pocket.

"I made sure the disc jockey didn't try anything funny," he went on. "I don't think either one of us is up to rap or heavy metal."

"I beg your pardon?"

"Charlie Simpson, the eighth-grade audiovisual aide," he explained. "I made sure he'd start the dance with a nice, slow song."

Impossibly dangerous, she thought.

"I can't dance," she said.

"Then a slow song is perfect. You don't have to dance. We'll just shuffle around for a few minutes."

Victoria lifted one eyebrow. In one respect, at least, he was like every other man she'd ever known: He had all the answers. While making him no less dangerous, it did make him seem more familiar.

With a show of spirit rather than submission, she yielded to Talbot custom and Ty Garrett's arms.

A spattering of applause greeted their move to the center of the gymnasium. Boys hooted and girls giggled. Victoria blushed. Ty turned her into the dance.

After wading through yards of material, his hand found the small of her back. He'd never felt cloth so light and soft. It moved under his hand like water, unresisting yet vibrant. The dress must be silk, he thought. He filled his hand with orange flowers and let them slide free. Silk. It brought sensual images to mind, of sheets and heat, of lingerie and bare skin, and of him crushing her to him and burying his face in the soft, wonderful curve of her neck.

"Mr. Garrett," she exclaimed softly.

"Excuse me," he said, his voice rougher than usual. He lightened his hold a degree, but not much more than that. He hadn't meant to crush her to him, but neither could he convince himself of the need to retreat. He liked her close. He liked holding her hand in his. He liked the way her dress brushed against his thighs.

"Where are you from, Mr. Garr—Ty?" Someone had once told Victoria that that question was a surefire conversation starter, and she desperately thought she and Mr. Garrett needed the addition of conversation to their dance, which was very slow indeed.

"I was born and raised on the Sky Canyon Ranch."

"How interesting," she said. "And where is the Sky Canyon Ranch?"

"About three miles due east of town. My parents are gone now, so Corey and I have the place to ourselves."

"You've never lived anywhere else?" She tilted her head back and gave him a quizzical look.

"Nope. The ranch has been in the family for four generations. My great-great-grandfather started raising horses and cattle in Texas after the

Civil War to get away from the carpetbaggers. We were Rebels," he said, grinning down at her.

She wasn't surprised.

"Then my great-grandfather got a hankering to see Colorado, and he trailed the herd north. We've been on the grassland ever since. The size and shape of the ranch has changed quite a few times, depending on drought and the price of cattle, or the price of land."

"Remarkable," she said, meaning it.

"How about you? Where are you from?"

"Everywhere and nowhere. I've been on every continent and in dozens of countries, but I can't truly call any of the places I've been 'home.' I never stayed anywhere long enough."

"Not even when you were in school?" A hint of surprise colored his voice.

"Oh, most definitely not. My education was more portable than I was."

"I heard you have a bunch of degrees," he said, making the statement close to a question.

Unexpectedly, she laughed. "Ah, yes, my degrees." She didn't sound nearly as impressed as the school board member who had told him all about them.

"I heard Oxford. Isn't that in England?"

"Yes, it is, and nicely endowed by the Willoughbys."

Ty hesitated to ask the question her information and her polite sarcasm brought to mind, but he did anyway. "Did your husband buy you a degree?"

"Goodness no!" She looked up at him, truly shocked. "One cannot *buy* a degree from Oxford." She paused for a moment, then added in an offhand manner, "But one can have certain inadequacies overlooked in light of certain strengths, if one has enough money and power behind them."

"Your husband was rich?"

"Quite," she said, then wished she hadn't. To the best of her ability, she tried not to drag her personal problems into her professional relationships, and Ty Garrett was a professional acquaintance. She hadn't told the school board or the administration about her battle with the Willoughby estate. There was certainly no reason to tell a young rancher who probably wouldn't understand the legal and moral intricacies of dealing with powerful, greedy progeny. She barely understood them herself.

She hazarded a quick glance at him. He caught her gaze and smiled. Her lashes immediately lowered to a less disturbing angle. Fortunately, he didn't seem inclined to press for the details of her husband's wealth and her near-penniless condition. He seemed content just to dance, and maybe he was right. Conversation hadn't been such a good idea after all. With very little effort, it had become quite personal.

On the other hand, conversation of any kind was preferable to having nothing to think about except their proximity. For a moment she'd forgotten they were touching, but with silence came awareness—sharp, clear, and uncomfortable in a way she was sure she shouldn't like.

Most notable was the consistency of his body. He was hard everywhere they touched. She'd never known anyone as strong or fit. His chest was an unrelenting wall against which her breasts were pressed. His arm claimed her waist like an iron band of possession, confident and unbreakable.

She'd never felt the power of flexed muscles the way Ty's muscles moved under his shirt and kept her within his arms. She'd never felt a broad, straight shoulder like the one under her hand. Held in his arms, feeling his strength, she couldn't help but wonder what he would look like without his shirt. Would he look like Michelangelo's *David*, the only naked young man she'd seen? Or would he look warmer, even more sensual because he was alive?

The latter, no doubt, she mused, despite the amazing firmness of his musculature. The only softness she found in Ty Garrett was the softness of his cheek touching her brow and the gentleness of his hand making lazy circles across her back.

She stiffened.

When had he started that? she wondered, startled at how easily she had accepted his unacceptable behavior. She took a careful breath. He really must stop, she thought, stop that slow slide of his fingers and palm down her spine and over the curve of her hip as he guided her through the motions of the dance.

How much guiding was necessary and how much was superfluous was a calculation she found herself unable to make. She didn't know what kind of dance they were doing. Conversation was her only hope.

"So, Mr. Garrett . . . I mean, Ty. Tell me about your schooling." Her voice sounded as faint as she felt.

As if he'd noticed the change, he tightened his hold on her, which didn't help. It didn't help at all.

"Well, I spent two years at Chadron State on a rodeo scholarship. Studied business, rodeoed hard, and went to Bozeman once for the college finals. I had a real good roping partner that year. He wanted to go pro, and we might have made some pretty fair money. We held our own on the college circuit, and were darn near unbeatable at amateur rodeos."

"Why didn't you go professional?" she asked, daring once again to look up at him.

He met her gaze, and a slow smile curved his mouth. "Corey. Mom and Dad were real good to let me have a couple of years of college, but he was my responsibility. Besides, I missed him, seeing him only summers and on weekends when I wasn't at a rodeo somewhere."

"What about your wife? Didn't she help out?" The inappropriateness of the question didn't occur to her until the words were out. But given the way he was touching her, it was a wonder she could think at all, let alone think in advance of speaking.

"I've never been married," he said, and came to a halt in the middle of the dance floor. His arm stayed securely around her waist.

"Oh, excuse me. I'm sorry. I mean—" Goodness, but their conversations got personal quickly.

"No need to be sorry. I don't think Linda and I could have made a go of it. She was only seventeen."

"Oh, yes. I see . . . The difficulty, that is . . ."

"And I was only eighteen. I wanted to marry

her, but our folks got together and decided that marriage probably wouldn't be the best thing."

"How terrible for you," Victoria said. After jumping feetfirst into a messy situation, she felt it was imperative she show her support. It was the only gracious thing to do after such a mortifying blunder. "I'm sure you must have loved her very much."

"I might have thought so once, but it didn't last long. She wanted to give the baby up for adoption."

Despite her best attempt at discretion, Victoria knew her shock showed. "I didn't think . . . Of course . . . usually it's the men . . ."

"I think her folks talked her into it. They wanted the best for her, a four-year college, a career, all the things they thought were important."

His casual discussion of the most intimate details of his life in no way relieved her own discomfort. And she couldn't imagine why he was confessing it all to her.

"A young girl . . . Yes, I see . . . Of course . . ."

"I hope this doesn't change the way you feel about Corey. He thinks you're great." For the first time, his face grew serious.

"Oh, no, Mr. Garrett," she rushed to assure

him. "Corey is a wonderful child, quite enough to make any parent proud. The complicated circumstances of his birth . . . Well, they wouldn't influence . . . or change the way I—I mean, he's a wonderful child," she ended on a lame note, chagrined at her own embarrassment.

"It wasn't all that complicated," he said, and the teasing grin he gave her made her pulse race. It also made her doubt that he was experiencing the same amount of humiliation she was, though the problem had most certainly been his and not hers.

"Of course not . . . I didn't mean . . ." She was flailing for words again.

"Things just got out of hand. You know how that can happen."

No. No, she didn't. She didn't know anything about it at all, except that she could understand how someone much younger and less mature than herself could possibly get out of hand with someone like Ty Garrett. But she wouldn't tell him that. She was already dumbstruck as it was.

"You know, Victoria," he said, his voice low and soft, his hand trailing along the curve of her chin. "If you didn't fluster so easily, and so prettily, I wouldn't enjoy doing it to you quite so much."

There came his grin again, and she felt herself

grow warm from her cheeks to the tips of her toes.

"However do you keep the high school boys from teasing you to death?" he asked, letting his thumb rub dangerously close to her bottom lip.

"They are not inclined, sir," she said, her words a bare whisper. Her reversion to the utmost formality did not discourage him, not one iota.

"And kissing?"

"They would never even *think* of such a thing," she said firmly.

"Oh, they're thinking it all right." His grin broadened, and he guided her back into the movements of the dance.

"They're mere children," she insisted.

"And you're naive, Oxford and all."

Actually, her naïveté was crumbling rather quickly under his teasing onslaught. A few stark, undeniable, and quite surprising realizations were taking its place, and once loosed, they were expounding and extrapolating at an alarming rate.

Simply put, his smile made her think of sex. Though given her experience, she couldn't imagine why. His smile was much too wonderful to be connected with those few furtive moments spent in the dark with Charles. Yet when he smiled, she thought of sex. The connection had been so unexpected, it had been a difficult one to make.

Every time he smiled, though, she thought of

kissing him in ways she'd never been kissed. She wasn't sure anybody kissed the way her imagination conjured up when he smiled, yet she still thought about running her tongue across his clean white teeth and holding his face in her hands. She thought about tasting him and touching him.

Truly, she'd never felt anything like it, this need to get closer. She thought she might like to dance with him for the rest of the night, and she was sure she didn't dare succumb to such foolishness.

A quick glance at him confirmed the reasonableness of her decision. At least as much trouble lay in his clear gray eyes as in his mouth. Long, thick lashes lent him an air of innocence, but his dark eyebrows made the innocence enticingly sensual. The irises themselves shone with brightness and warmth, giving him a particularly playful look. Now that she'd been forced to the bare truth, there was no doubt.

Playful sensuality. Until she'd met him, she would have thought the two words incompatible. She'd never known anyone playful, and certainly no one sensual. In truth, she'd never known anyone like Ty Garrett. He exhibited heretofore undocumented characteristics.

No wonder he disturbed her. No wonder at all.

FOUR

Victoria survived the dance with little more than her duty intact. Talbot custom and Ty Garrett's arms had proven near disastrous to her emotions and her wits. Stationing herself by the fruit-punch dispenser, she vowed to take the rest of the evening more firmly in hand and not to budge unless it proved absolutely necessary.

"Miss Willoughby?" Claire Clark, one of her students, came up to her, looking worried and nervous. "Can I stand here next to you? Bobby Palmer is after me to dance, and I don't want to dance with him."

"Certainly, Claire," Victoria said, pleased she had regained her image of quiet control. Bobby Palmer was brash, bigger than anybody else in the whole junior high, and had enough other masculine attributes to make any thirteen-year-old girl nervous. "Would you like some punch?"

"Please." Claire huddled closer, her finger busily twisting together long strands of her honey-blond hair. The girl was pretty and relied on the fact more than Victoria thought was wise, given the impermanence of youthful beauty. Charles had often praised her for her own quick mind, telling her it was the one asset she could depend on to pull her through any situation. To date he'd been right—barring any situation that included Ty Garrett.

Feeling her composure slipping, Victoria quickly turned and began filling a paper cup with punch. Ty Garrett had no business lingering in her thoughts. The dance was over.

"*Miss Willoughby!*" Claire shrieked under her breath, and grabbed for an arm to hold.

The punch cup and Victoria's chest collided with a quick jerk and a splash. She sucked in her breath while red punch soaked into her beige trellises and orange poppies, leaving a huge, garish splotch down the front of her dress.

"He's coming *over!*" Claire squealed, oblivious to the disaster she'd caused.

With effort Victoria controlled her anger and irritation. "Calm down, Claire. I'll handle Bobby

Palmer." She picked up a paper napkin and dabbed at her dress. It was hopeless.

"Not Bobby," Claire said, her voice full of excitement. "*Ty Garrett* is coming over."

Victoria froze in mid-dab. She looked over her shoulder and swallowed hard. Ty Garrett was indeed coming over. She would rather have faced ten Bobby Palmers.

"Gawd, he's so cute." Claire gushed and giggled while Victoria fought panic. She didn't deserve this night.

Grabbing more napkins, she made a hasty attempt to pull herself together. She dabbed top to bottom and left to right, then once again all over, fast.

"Victoria?"

Her heart missed a beat. She whirled around with the giant wad of napkins pressed to her chest.

"Mr. Garrett?" She lifted her chin to meet his eyes, forcing calmness into her voice.

"Ty," he insisted, smiling. Then his gaze fell on the napkins and the splotch. Concern lifted his eyes back to hers. "What happened?"

"Hi, Ty," Claire said, sidling between them. Unconcealed adoration softened her voice and put a totally inappropriate sultriness in her movements.

Victoria looked askance at the suddenly flirtatious young woman. Whatever was the girl thinking? she wondered, then on second thought decided she didn't want to know. Not when Claire was only thirteen and Mr. Garrett—Ty—was . . . was so close.

"Hi, Claire," he said, taking Victoria's arm. "Could you excuse us for a minute?"

He didn't wait for an answer as he grabbed a handful of napkins and pulled her a little farther down the snack table.

"I should have warned you about the kids getting rowdy," he said in apology. "Somebody is always spilling something on somebody at these dances. I'm sorry it was you."

Victoria allowed herself to be guided to the end of the table, thinking it was terribly gallant of him to assume she hadn't ruined her own dress.

"It was an accident," she assured him. "The young person was momentarily distracted." A female reaction she was beginning to understand with startling clarity. Ty Garrett was the most physically distracting man she'd ever met. She would never forget how strong and solid his thighs had felt against her when they'd danced. She was sure she would want to forget, but she knew she wouldn't.

They stopped in front of the chips and dip, and his eyes met hers, serious and beautifully gray. He had sinful lashes, so thick and dark and long.

"Was it Bobby Palmer? I saw him hanging around, and I—" He absently lifted the handful of napkins toward her, and their conversation came to a sudden, not-so-absent halt.

What in the world was he thinking of doing with those napkins? she wondered, her pulse picking up.

Ty caught her reaction and wondered the same thing. What had he been thinking? That he would press a few flimsy pieces of paper and his hand to her breast? His gaze followed his thoughts and his chest grew tight. He'd meant no disrespect, he was sure. But he knew from dancing with her that her dress was deceiving when it came to her anatomy. Her breasts were full and lush, and they were rising and falling in a quickening rhythm, another signal bound to keep him awake most of the night.

The thought brought his head up, and his gaze collided with that of his son. Corey was giving him a look of desperate encouragement from across the gymnasium, as if he knew half the battle had been lost but that there was still hope.

Ty felt a compelling urge to go over to Corey and explain that he hadn't been the one to spill fruit punch all over Miss Willoughby's dress.

That he hadn't forgotten Corey's advice, and that he also hadn't stepped on her when they'd danced. And that there was no reason to call Lacey, because his father was well able to handle himself and one not very troublesome, but somehow incredibly disconcerting woman.

"I'll have a talk with Bobby," he said, lowering his arm and dropping the napkins on the table as discreetly as possible. He'd been in control once this evening, when they'd been dancing, and he swore he'd get her to dance with him again—no matter what it took.

Victoria released her breath in an audible sigh, not caring if he heard her or not. She was too relieved to care. For a moment he'd been about to touch her intimately, and her whole body had come alive in a dizzying, dangerous rush.

"It wasn't Bobby." She sounded breathless, and she didn't care if he knew that either. The man was a mine field. She needed to get away from him. She took a step backward. She needed some distance between her and his eyes, his body, his smile. She took another step—and the potato chip bowl crashed to the floor.

Embarrassment flooded through her. It was too much. She'd never been clumsy. Economy and efficiency of movement had been ingrained in her right along with the economy and efficiency of all other aspects of her life.

An unrelenting sense of responsibility forced her to her knees to pick up chips, when all she wanted to do was run for cover. Worse yet, Ty Garrett's sense of responsibility sent him to the floor with her.

"My fault," he said, sweeping broken chips into a pile with his hands.

"No . . . really. I bumped into the table."

Their knees were almost touching, his right and her left, and their heads were bowed together over the small mess. Victoria wished he'd left her alone to clean up. His help was more disturbing than useful.

"I know," he said, "but that was my fault, too. I make you nervous."

The boldness of his statement left her speechless. She slowly raised her head and found him smiling at her. The gentleness of the expression shone in his eyes and in the shallow creases of his sun-browned cheeks. Her gaze unexpectedly lowered to his mouth. His bottom lip was slightly fuller than the top one, his teeth white and straight. As she stared, his smile faded, and before she realized what was happening, he leaned forward and kissed her.

The caress of his mouth on hers was brief and

potent, with only a heartbeat of time between his nose brushing against hers and his sigh blowing across her lips in retreat. It was the sigh that shook her to the core. More than the touch of his mouth, his sigh was filled with yearning and promise. He'd not only kissed her, he'd wanted to kiss her very badly.

"I came over to tell you I have to go out in the parking lot and help get a truck started," he said, filling the huge void of shocked silence with his soft, easy drawl and commonplace words.

"By all means," she said, her voice a bare whisper, her encouragement sincere. The parking lot was the best place for him. She needed to think, and as it stood, with him so near, her thought processes had completely shut down. She was running on automatic pilot alone.

He'd kissed her.

"I shouldn't be gone very long. Sounds like he only needs a jump. If you need me, send one of the kids out."

"Of course." She knew all about jumper cables and the combustion engine. She did not know much about kissing. Ty Garrett did it similarly to Charles, but with a difference she didn't comprehend. The action was the same, the quick touching of mouths. Charles had sometimes pressed a bit harder, a little less comfortably against her.

The sigh had been unique though. And her response had been unprecedented, including the time of her unmentionable indiscretion. The kiss of her indiscretion had gone physically further than Ty Garrett's, yet not as emotionally far as a sigh.

"I'm sorry about your dress," he said.

"Oh, don't be, really. I was never quite sure it was right for me."

He flashed her a grin and took her hand in his, helping her to her feet. "And I was just getting to like it."

She nodded, as if it were only natural for him to like her dress better after it had fruit punch spilled down the front and dozens of potato-chip crumbs clinging to the hem.

When he walked away, she turned and braced herself on the snack table, closing her eyes and taking a deep, head-clearing breath. But her head didn't clear, not at all. He'd kissed her, and everything inside her was acutely aware, buzzing with life and the memories of the seconds when he'd touched his mouth to hers.

She would be the first to admit she'd led a sheltered life: growing up all over the world in the company of a group of much older, highly academic men. Men who had little or no time to spend on a young girl's curiosity about anything other than the historically or scientifically significant subject at hand. She knew she'd missed some of the finer points of the male-female relationship, and her years with Charles had done little to enlighten her. There had been no abuse, of course, sexual, emotional, verbal, or otherwise. She and Charles had been above anything as personally involved as abuse. Sex had been a chore, kissing a duty, affection rare. Even physically they'd been as unattached as possible.

But Ty Garrett had kissed her, and she felt longing. He had sighed against her lips, and she felt wanted. She knew those two emotions, with little effort, could change her life forever, make her something other than what she was.

The very idea scared her senseless.

Ty had to get by without a second dance with Victoria Willoughby. There had been no helping it. The evening had gone on a downhill slide after the first dance, and he'd been unable to do anything except go along for the ride and pick up the pieces.

For starters, Josie Brannerman had gotten sick, and the Gibson boy had gotten scraped up and bruised. Victoria had held the girl's hand until the teenager's mother had been able to get into town and take her home. Ty had sat the boy down, administered first aid, and explained to him that most girls weren't impressed by how many bleacher seats a boy could jump. The feat impressed the hell out of other boys, but girls didn't take much stock in bleacher-seat jumping.

Then Victoria had caught one of the eighth-graders chewing tobacco and had given him a lecture while she'd marched him to the bathroom. She'd made Ty go in after him to make sure the boy rinsed out his mouth.

Later Ty had followed a commotion out to the parking lot and chased off a group of high school boys, after checking to make sure they didn't have any junior high school girls with them.

To top things off, the sound system had died about three-quarters of the way through the dance. Ty had spent a good half hour fixing it, then listened in discouragement as it gave up the ghost a second time.

And through it all ran the inevitable heart-breaks. Some girls were never asked to dance, some boys were never accepted as partners. New romances began. Old romances died messy deaths amid the confusion of adolescent emotions.

The one positive note of the evening was an overnight invitation from Corey's best friend. Ty had agreed without hesitation, then had spent the rest of the evening wondering if Corey had arranged the invitation so Ty could be alone with Miss Willoughby when he took her home, in case he got a signal. He appreciated the opportunity, but he liked to think he could manage such things on his own.

When the time came, though, his gratitude far outweighed his concern. He brought his truck to a slow stop in her gravel driveway, shut off the ignition, and turned to face her.

"Thanks for helping out with the dance," he said, knocking his hat back on his head and draping one arm over the steering wheel. She'd been quiet on the short ride home. After all the noise and ruckus of the dance, he hadn't blamed her, or missed the conversation. But he didn't want the evening to end just yet. "We should be safe from Glen Frazer up until about Christmas. He's usually looking for plenty of help around the holidays."

"Thanks for the warning," she said, glancing at him from her side of the truck cab. A deep breath followed her statement, then she reached for the door. "And thanks for the dance—I mean the evening—and your help."

"My pleasure," he said, watching her hand on the door latch and wondering whether he should reach for her or let her go. "The last time I chaperoned was with Ann Riverson, and she's not nearly as pretty as you."

Victoria felt a blush warming her cheeks, not at all sure his words were complimentary. Ann Riverson put new meaning into the word "spinster," and Victoria had often wondered if a few more years of her own would have her ending up looking as pinched and dried out as the Talbot English teacher.

"Miss Riverson is a very good teacher," she said in her colleague's defense.

"So are you," he countered. "And you're still pretty."

A definite compliment, she decided, her blush deepening.

"Mr. Garrett," she began.

"Ty."

"Mr. Garrett." She looked up and held his gaze. "It's been a rather remarkable evening. I've never had one quite like it, and I—"

"We could do it again," he interrupted. "I would like to take you someplace where we didn't have fifty kids to look after. Or, for that matter, fifty kids looking after us." A grin broke across his face, filled with a teasing promise she didn't dare acknowledge, because it brought to mind the same longing she'd felt with his kiss.

"No, thank you," she said quickly before she

gave in to his smile and herself. "And thank you again." She opened the door and made a move to leave, but he reached for her.

The pressure of his hand on her arm was slight, barely there, but it was enough to freeze her into immobility.

"I'd like to see you again," Ty said, going for broke.

"I'm sure we'll see each other, Mr. Garrett. Talbot is quite small and—"

"If it was the kiss, I could apologize."

Her crestfallen gaze flicked up to meet his. The moment passed almost instantly, but not before Ty received and analyzed the signal inherent in her dismay.

"I wouldn't want to," he said quickly. "Apologize, that is, for kissing you. Not when it wasn't my fault. And I liked it too much for you to apologize to me."

"I beg your pardon?" She stiffened under his hand.

"I was more than ready to oblige when you asked me to kiss you," he explained.

"Asked?"

"Asked." His grin returned in full force.

"Mr. Garrett, let me assure you, I never asked you to kiss me or anybody else. Not one word of such a request ever—"

"You didn't say it out loud."

"*Of course I didn't,*" she said, thoroughly shocked.

"But you were looking at my mouth, and the way you were looking made me think of kissing."

Her gaze inadvertently slipped down to his smile, and she remembered. His lips had been warm, his breath so soft blowing against her skin. "I—I can't be held responsible for your imagination."

"You're doing it again."

A guilty blush colored her cheeks. He moved closer, and she slowly lifted her gaze to meet his eyes.

"No doubt about it, Miss Willoughby," he drawled, leaning over her. "When you look at me like that, I get to thinking about kissing."

She could have slipped away and gotten out of the truck. He gave her plenty of time. She could have pushed him back, or she could have told him to refrain from whatever in the world he was thinking about doing this time.

She did nothing.

Curiosity was an academic virtue she endeavored to instill in her students, and she was powerfully curious about Ty Garrett's kiss. His mouth came down on hers, easy and gentle, demanding nothing more than that he be allowed to touch her lips with his own. She granted him the favor of one chaste kiss. There could be no harm, she told herself, in a single kiss.

No harm, at least, in a chaste kiss. But the first thing she learned was the inevitable tendency of a kiss to change. From one second to the next, the kiss was different from the way it had been before and, as she quickly realized, not the same as it was going to be. The soft stroke of his tongue across her lips surprised and alarmed her. It also sent a melting sweetness rippling down her body. She sighed without meaning to, and he deepened the kiss, taking advantage of her response.

Suddenly Victoria's imagination had nothing on reality. Ty ran his tongue over her teeth, then turned her tighter into his arms and softly plundered her mouth. Fascination warred with propriety— and fascination won.

Comparisons between the kiss and any other she'd ever received were impossible. There were no similarities. Certainly none she could catalogue fast enough to keep up with the changes he kept instigating, except possibly the same edge of excitement she'd felt when he'd briefly kissed her by the potato chips. Except this time the excitement was sharper, more needy, and totally irresistible.

He kissed with an intimacy that was astonishing, wet and hot, and more personal than anything she'd done with Charles. She pressed herself against the truck seat and clenched fistfuls of her dress. He had a power unlike any she'd ever felt, seductive in its intensity, with passion as its goal. She wanted him to kiss her forever.

Ty thought forever might be what it would take for her to relax. Her mouth was sweetly compliant, soft, and submissive, but the rest of her body was as stiff as a board. He didn't know whether to press her for more or back away. Not that he wasn't thoroughly enamored of the status quo. Her mouth *was* sweet, shy, and tender, and every small response he got went simultaneously to his head and his groin.

Kissing her brought him more pleasure than he'd expected, deep down and erotically enticing despite the hesitation in her every move. He began to remember just exactly what it was he'd been missing about women all this time. He began to think he wanted Miss Willoughby more than was reasonable or wise.

He slanted his mouth across hers, hoping for a bit more of a reaction. When he got it, he made up his mind: Victoria Willoughby would be his.

Victoria wouldn't have believed anyone who told her the kiss could get even better, closer, hotter. But when he sealed his mouth over hers, cupped her face in his palm, and began a slow, thorough seduction of her mouth, she recognized the difference and his intent without a doubt clouding her judgment. Ty Garrett's smile had made her think of sex for a very good reason. He was doing nothing less than making love to her with his kiss. Inviting mouth, indeed. Everything about his mouth was a blatant invitation to abandonment . . . sensual abandonment. Suddenly, beyond the pleasure and excitement, beyond the curiosity she was sure would never be satisfied when it came to him, she felt panic welling up inside her.

Ty felt it too. She gave him a hundred signals in her quick retreat from the kiss. He slowly lifted his head and inhaled a deep, calming breath. But he didn't relinquish his dominant position of leaning over her with her half in his arms.

"I would like to take you out to dinner next Saturday night." His voice was rough and soft at the same time.

When she didn't respond, except to look at him through her big round glasses with wide-eyed disbelief, he kissed her again carefully.

"Please come with me, Victoria." His mouth touched hers once more. "I don't get the chance to get out very much, and it would mean a lot if you would have dinner with me."

He started to kiss her again, but Victoria was positive she was at her limit. Any more kisses and she refused to be responsible for herself.

"Yes," she said quickly, before he could get any closer. "An evening out would be lovely, I'm sure."

A slow, easy grin spread across his face just before he leaned down and kissed her one more time, literally kissing her senseless, she was sure. It was the only explanation she could come up with for her actions, and she'd be the first to admit it wasn't very damned scientific.

FIVE

"Out of the frying pan and into the fire" was a quaint saying Victoria had never dreamed she would be using to describe a predicament of her own making. Yet that was exactly what she'd done by agreeing to go out on a real date with Ty Garrett—jumped right out of the frying pan and into the fire.

She jerked her skirt around, trying it with the zipper in the back instead of on the side. Clothing was designed to fit a certain way, and there were supposed to be clues, like tags and darts. Her skirt had darts everywhere, and the tags were about halfway down a seam, giving her no clue whatsoever as to which panel was the back. She'd always worn the skirt however it happened to go on, but that wasn't good enough for tonight. She wanted to get it right. Just once, please.

Dissatisfied with what she saw in the mirror, she whipped the skirt completely around, trying the totally daring position of having the zipper in front. She stepped back, looked, and was glad no one else was in the room with her.

She tried the left side. She tried the right side. She tried the back once more, all the while smoothing the skirt with her hands in the hopes she could get out the lumps.

The material was beautiful and quite expensive, a foresty green with a nubby brown weft. Or maybe it was a warp. Regardless, the wool of her suit had come from only the finest sheep, been woven in the finest mills, and been sewn by the finest seamstresses for a Willoughby Victoria had never met, but who Charles had assured her felt beholden to send more clothes along for his wife. Victoria just needed to improve her posture to make the clothes fit.

She straightened her shoulders, pulled in her stomach, and decided on keeping the zipper in the back. She just hoped a suit wasn't too formal for a dinner date.

Ty had been ready for anything, or so he'd thought. When Victoria opened her door, though, he was seized by an urgent desire to do away with her clothes. To gather up some of the suit jacket and make it less huge, to somehow straighten the ill-fitting wrinkles out of her skirt, and, if possible, to change the muddy-green color of the outfit. The only nice thing about the suit was that it covered up most of an awful yellow blouse.

She was so pretty. He didn't understand how she could have ended up with nothing but big, ugly clothes. None of the women he knew had ever had the luxury of being clotheshorses, but even Lacey fussed around with herself until she achieved a flattering look.

"Hi," he said, smiling. The suit be damned, he was glad to see her. He'd thought about little else all week.

"Come in. Please." She opened the door wider and gestured for him to enter. "I'll be only a minute. I just have to feed my cat."

It was a lie.

Victoria had prepared herself for the moment of Ty Garrett's arrival, but with it upon her, she found she needed either more preparation or more moments. So she asked him in, voiced her polite lie, and left him on his own while she beat a hasty retreat to the kitchen.

There was a cat she could feed, but it most definitely wasn't hers. The stray tom showed up when he pleased, did as he pleased, and was particularly pompous as he went about pleasing himself. In short, he was a familiar male presence, unlike the one standing in her living room, looking tall and dark, very masculine, undeniably handsome, and quintessentially western from the top of his black cowboy hat to the toes of his fancy leather boots.

"Archie, kitty, kitty," she called out the back door, shaking a milk carton for added incentive. Within seconds she was miraculously rewarded with a responsive yowl.

A sleek orange and white feline streaked past her into the kitchen, giving her all the excuse she needed to dawdle until she was ready to face her date. She promised herself she wouldn't take more than a couple of minutes. She didn't want to make a fool of herself. She just wanted a chance to shore up her composure, a chance to calm herself, a chance to reclaim a mature perspective on the last time she'd seen him, up close and personal, after he had ravished her with his kiss.

Ty mosied around the living room, looking at photographs and books. She had a lot of both. The house itself belonged to the school district. Depending on the individual teaching contract, it was sometimes offered rent-free, or at a reduced rent. Sometimes the board threw in free propane. Ty had heard that they had offered Victoria the works, every benefit the district had or could dig up, and that they still felt like they'd gotten the bargain of the century.

Looking at the framed degrees, certificates, and awards covering one of the living room walls, he agreed. He was impressed and a little taken aback by what all the flowing script had to say about the woman in the kitchen. She must have studied at half the universities in the world.

He walked over to the desk beneath the living room window and let his gaze roam over the haphazardly arranged photographs: Victoria in front of the pyramids, with older men on either side of her; a much younger Victoria with a satchel, standing in front of an awesomely gothic building; Victoria on a barge, flanked by the same old men; a portrait of one of the men, a head and shoulders shot. Balding head and stooped shoulders.

Ty picked up the picture, then turned when she entered the room. Their eyes met, but only for a second before her gaze shifted to his mouth. He grinned, and her startled gaze flew back to his eyes.

She did wonderful things for his ego. Corey and Lacey could rest assured he had the situation firmly in hand.

"It's . . . uh, Charles," she said, directing

his attention back to the photograph in his hand. "It was taken a few months before he died, for inclusion in the Willoughby Institute directory. We have a number of highly prominent people in the organization."

Her husband? Ty looked down at the photograph, noticing what he'd casually overlooked before, like the gray color of what little hair Charles had had left, the sallowness of his skin, a slackness around the man's mouth, and the years—decades of them—etched into the lines of the man's face and the weariness of his eyes.

He didn't know what to say. Fortunately she saved him the effort of finding something.

"He was quite brilliant."

"Yeah." Ty put the photograph back on the desk. "I think you mentioned that at Parents' Night. He was a colleague of your father's, wasn't he? And your teacher?"

"Yes. After my father died, Charles took me under his wing." A small sigh escaped her. "He wasn't at all well the last year or so. He died in Buenos Aires. We were doing research on pampean grasslands."

How exotic, Ty thought, and how incredibly old her husband had been for her. But Ty had figured out the mystery of her wardrobe. If he had been an old man married to a pretty young woman, he would have hidden her under a lot of brown, baggy clothes too.

"I'm sorry," he said. "That must have been hard for you, being so far from home." He'd finally found something correct to say.

"Actually, I wasn't any farther from home than usual. That wasn't the hard part."

Ty was quickly getting in over his head, and with any other woman he would have backed off from the conversation. But he didn't with Victoria. He didn't know why she wanted to tell him about her husband's death, but if she wanted to talk, he was willing to listen.

"He had three children by a previous marriage," she explained, stepping over to the desk and rearranging a few of the pictures. "They are all older than me by quite a bit."

The information did not surprise him, not after seeing the photograph.

"When Charles died, they swooped down on our apartment in Argentina and took over everything, including our research. I've been rather out in the cold ever since."

"That's why you're not rich anymore?"

"Yes," she said simply.

"He should have taken better care of you." Ty knew it wasn't any of his business, but he found he didn't like her dead husband.

"I thought so at first."

"What changed your mind?" he asked, setting the photograph aside and trying to hide his irritation. He wasn't in much of a forgiving mood when it came to old Charles Edward Willoughby IV.

A moment passed before she answered.

"For the first time in my life I'm responsible for taking care of myself. I like it. The more they take away from me, the less I seem to need. I'm getting along quite well without servants, though I do sometimes miss my secretary. J.J. could grade all those homework papers, do my lesson plans, keep Mr. Frazer happy, and still have energy left over to work on organizing my research."

Ty stared at her, his eyes narrowing in a moment of disbelief, as if he expected her to laugh and tell him she'd only been joking. But she didn't. Servants and secretaries. He wondered just how rich old Charles had been. Richer than Ty had thought, that was for damn sure.

"My grassland research is on hold," she continued, "but I plan on resuming it next summer on the Pawnee. I've become quite intrigued with the Buffalo Commons idea, whether or not the Great Plains, if left alone to rejuvenate itself, could once again support a free-ranging buffalo herd comparable to the wildebeest herds on the Serengeti and Masai Mara."

That jerked him out of his wondering reverie. "You're kidding," he said, hoping she was even as he sincerely doubted it.

"Not in the least," she assured him, a small smile curving the corners of her mouth. "I think it is one of the grandest ideas I've ever come across."

"What about the ranchers already out here trying to make a living?" Ty had heard about the Buffalo Commons idea, and he thought it was grand all right. Grandly crazy.

"Certain sacrifices will have to be made, of course."

Ty agreed, but begged to differ on who should have to make the sacrifices. The difference of opinion and the ensuing conversation got them to the restaurant a half hour away without a single awkward moment. Even so, Ty was aware that once again an evening with Victoria Willoughby had gotten off on an unexpected, strangely intimate note.

Victoria was also quite aware of this turn of events and was equally at a loss as to how to explain it. She did take full responsibility for revealing the circumstances of her financial situation. But she still didn't understand why she had—unless it had something to do with Ty's kiss. Possibly, such physical intimacy had triggered her outburst of personal facts.

Then again, there had been his unexpected confessions on the dance floor. Maybe those had loosened her own tongue. Maybe Ty Garrett was going to be a friend. She slanted him a quick glance and felt her cheeks warm. Her money was on the kiss.

Ty had chosen his favorite restaurant, the Red Lantern. On arrival he realized it hadn't been his wisest decision. To begin with, because of its proximity to Talbot, it was everybody's favorite restaurant. Greg and Amy Lambert were pulling up at the same time as Ty and Victoria. Ty wasn't surprised, and he wasn't pleased, and he wished he'd remembered that most Saturday nights at the Lantern looked like a Talbot homecoming.

He returned Greg's greeting and waved across the parking lot. With a little less enthusiasm he included Amy. He didn't want to be rude, but neither did he want to encourage Amy. Not that she needed encouraging. She'd been at it again last Sunday, making eyes at him in church, brushing up against him in the Sunday school hallway, being coy and provocative at the same time, and consequently getting him to thinking about Victoria's kiss and a whole lot of other things he shouldn't have been thinking about.

He'd had a hell of a week, and all he wanted was to get Victoria off somewhere by himself, during dinner and after dinner. Especially after dinner. He did not want to spend the evening with Greg and Amy Lambert. Too late, he realized he should have told somebody out loud and in no uncertain terms.

He should have said, "Nice to see you, but Victoria and I want to be alone while we eat our supper. Just the two of us, her and me, not you. We don't want company."

If that had failed to get his point across, he should have said, "Go away, far away. Go on, *git!*"

He should not have been polite and subtle. Politeness had been taken as an overt act of friendship and subtleness as an invitation. By the time all the introductions had been made, his romantic dinner for two had become a party of four.

He put his hand on Victoria's back as they crossed the parking lot, trying to find a way to tell her a double date was not what he'd had planned. Trying hard, too, to resist taking her back out to his truck and heading on down the road to the next watering hole. Greg opened the door to the restaurant before he accomplished the first objective or gave in to the second.

"This is wonderful," Amy said, crowding

against him by the hostess desk. "The four of us having dinner together and all. It's always more fun to eat with friends. Don't you think so, Ty?"

"Sure, but—" He was still hoping to head a foursome off at the pass, but Amy was too quick for him.

She turned to Victoria with an overly bright smile. "I've heard so much about you, but every time I've seen you, you've always been busy with some school thing. This will be a wonderful chance for us to chat. Is it true your husband was of royal blood?"

"Charles was the Earl of Wickham," Victoria explained, "part of the nobility, not royalty."

"This is great, incredible," Amy said, her excitement growing more sincere. "Who would have guessed I'd ever have dinner with someone who has slept with the nobility?"

Ty didn't think it was so damn great, and he couldn't have imagined worse phrasing if he'd tried. Amy Lambert was quickly getting on his nerves, and not in that pleasant, arousing way he'd been allowing these last few weeks in church.

"That's a novel way of putting it . . . I suppose," Victoria said, looking as unsure as those little burrowing owlets had looked standing in the rain last spring. Ty's annoyance with Amy picked up in intensity.

"I have your table ready." The hostess returned and picked up a few menus. "If you'll follow me, please."

Ty's manners got him in trouble again at the table. He took a moment to hold Victoria's chair for her, and while he was busy, Amy and Greg commandeered the two seats on either side of her. He was left with the chair farthest away from his date. Apparently the status of the Lambert marriage was about what Ty had surmised from all of Amy's flirting.

"Should we order a pitcher of margaritas?" Amy asked. "Since there's four of us, I think that's the best way to go."

"Margaritas?" Victoria said, looking down at her menu.

"Sure," Greg said. "But they have to be on the rocks, none of that frozen stuff."

"Sure," Ty said. "Rocks."

"Margaritas?" Victoria repeated. Her menu had a silhouette of a carriage being drawn by four horses on the cover, with red lanterns and a driver in a top hat. It did not look like the sort of menu from which one went about ordering pitchers of margaritas.

"You've never had a margarita?" Amy asked, touching Victoria's arm and giving her a you-poor-thing-I-can't-believe-it look.

"Well, yes, I have," Victoria answered.

"Order whatever you like, Victoria," Ty said, reaching across the table and giving her hand a small squeeze. "I'm sure the three of us can handle a pitcher."

"No. A margarita will be fine," Victoria said, retrieving her hand and putting on a brave front. With a show of nonchalance she opened her menu, expecting the worst. Her expectations were met. Mexican food, the culinary bane of her existence. She didn't know which spice or combination of spices in Mexican cooking caused her to break out in a rash, but she knew enough to stay away from anything with a sauce.

She lifted her chin a degree higher and perused the menu. She would muddle through as she always had. Charles had loved Mexican food. The preference had been the single most surprising thing about him, his one streak of nonconformity.

She was not alone in her muddling. Ty felt as if he were muddling through the whole dinner too. Watching Victoria push her food around her plate just about killed his own appetite. The Red Lantern was locally famous for the quality of its food, but Victoria sure didn't look as though she were enjoying hers.

"Did you live in a castle?" Amy asked Victoria. By Ty's count, it was stupid question number fourteen.

"No. The Willoughbys have a large estate in Kent, but there's no castle."

"A large estate, how wonderful. You must be eager to get back," Amy said. "Talbot must be boring you to death."

"I haven't had time to be bored," Victoria said, ignoring Amy's other comment. She couldn't go back to Wickham. It now belonged to Charles's eldest son, Neville, and she most certainly was not on his social calendar, let alone his guest list.

"Lots of women don't have time to be bored." Greg entered the conversation with a pointed look at his wife. "Victoria probably has her hands full teaching all day."

Amy studiously ignored him, speaking again to Victoria. "Do all the clothes in England look like yours?"

Stupid question number fifteen. Ty wondered what Greg would do if he stuffed an enchilada into Amy's mouth. A whole enchilada.

Victoria glanced down at her suit, not at all sure what Amy Lambert meant. "Wool suits, possibly, look similar to mine in that they . . . um, would be made of wool." What *did* the woman mean? she wondered, then wished she hadn't when Amy supplied the answer.

"I mean the colors. Is it because of all the rain and fog that you wear such muddy colors? Nothing fresh and sunny. You know," she finished as if Victoria did know. But she didn't.

"I'm not sure," she said, managing at least to voice a lack of opinion. Amy Lambert's outfit was white and pink, quite bright and "sunny"-looking. But Thanksgiving was only two weeks away. So wasn't Amy's dress out of season? Victoria thought it might be, but, of course, being muddy-looking seemed by far the greater fashion sin.

Ty wasn't any good at defusing female animosity. He hadn't had enough practice. He wanted to come to Victoria's defense, but he didn't know how to do it without making things seem worse than they were.

"I like your suit," Greg said bluntly, surprising them all. "The wool is real high quality. Must have cost a fortune." He fingered the sleeve of Victoria's jacket. "And it's not muddy-looking. It's forest green and brown. Good colors."

"Thank you." Victoria practically beamed at the other man, and Ty wished he'd said he liked her suit. He didn't like it, but it would have been nice if he'd thought quickly enough to say it.

Greg grinned back at her. "I raised sheep

when I was a kid. Took them to the stock show a couple of times."

"How interesting," Victoria said. "A number of my students are involved in animal husbandry projects. I've told them they can submit their records for extra credit."

"Good idea. I remember keeping track of feeding and immunizations, grading the wool, all sorts of stuff."

Ty leaned back and watched as the conversation between his date and his neighbor took off as though they'd known each other for years. Hell, his whole life was one big animal husbandry project called ranching, but he hadn't thought to go talking cows to her. If he'd known it would get her smiling at him the way she was smiling at Greg, he would have talked cows to her all night long.

Instead, he'd argued buffalo, he reminded himself. They hadn't had a real argument, not like what Amy had been angling for, but buffalo talk hadn't gotten Victoria to batting her eyelashes the way he would swear she was doing at Greg. He wondered if the difference was between buffalo and sheep, or if it was between him and Greg. He wondered if he should mention his ranch and his ideas on crossbreeding. He wondered what that look on Amy's face meant, and he wondered if the night was going to get any worse.

SIX

Victoria thought dinner had gone without a hitch, except for the food being inedible, Amy Lambert being unfathomable, and a few extra tantalizing highlights she couldn't keep from analyzing and reanalyzing. Ty had put his hand on the small of her back as they'd crossed the parking lot to the restaurant. He had actually put his arm around her waist when the hostess had led them to their table. Twice during dinner he'd picked up her hand and briefly held it in his own. When they'd left the restaurant, he'd put her coat on her and practically held her in his arms.

Victoria had been literally warmed by the intimacy of the gesture. Halfway back to Talbot, she was still warm, and quite hungry, and she had come to a certain surprising but nonetheless supportable supposition: The man couldn't keep his hands off her.

She'd never felt so alluring, or so incredulous. Maybe the zipper did belong in the back, and maybe Amy Lambert had no more fashion sense than Victoria did herself. She was looking forward to analyzing that possibility over food, any kind of food, as soon as she got home.

Still, enough was enough. Try as she might, she couldn't see a future in Ty Garrett's touches and her surprising effect on him. She wasn't given to casual dalliances—despite what Charles had said after her indiscretion. The estate was bound to come out of probate with at least a portion of her bequest intact, and then she would be leaving Talbot to resume her duties as co-founder of the Willoughby Institute. It was the path she'd chosen for herself.

The smart thing was to put an end to what she was sure would remain one of the more intriguing interludes in her life. Ty Garrett was far too disturbing, too disconcerting, too dangerous, too enticing. She would put an end to it, and that would be that.

Of course, such a delicate subject should be approached with the utmost decorum and, if possible, roundabout grace.

"I enjoyed meeting your friends," she said. "It was nice of Greg to offer his help with the science fair."

Ty grunted.

Wordless masculine communication, namely grunting, was a language Victoria was all too familiar with; so much so that she hardly noticed Ty's lack of a more formally voiced response.

"Any help is appreciated," she continued. "But I wouldn't like the school board to think I can't handle it by myself. What do you think?"

Ty thought Greg had no business sashaying around Victoria like a moth hell-bent on getting burned. He thought Amy had been about to tell her husband just that in no uncertain terms. He thought Victoria had no idea how outrageously Greg had been flirting with her, though he'd gotten the impression Greg knew just exactly how outrageously his wife had been flirting with Ty all these Sundays past. He thought the date had been a disaster so far, and he was desperately trying to think of a way to salvage the evening and keep Greg Lambert from moving in on Victoria. The Lamberts were married, for crying out loud. Somebody should tell them to start acting like it.

He didn't say any of those things. A better idea, the perfect solution, suddenly came to mind.

"I'll help out too," he said, his mood immediately lifting. "We'll call it community involvement. The school board loves community involvement." He was already too busy by half, but somehow he would fit in the science fair. Glen Frazer would probably ask him for help anyway.

"What a wonderful idea. Thank you," Victoria said, then realized she shouldn't have. Foolish girl. A woman did not "break off" with a man by accepting his help.

They slipped back into a silence that grew more comfortable for Ty and less comfortable for Victoria as the minutes and the miles rolled by. Ty had effectively neutralized Greg Lambert. Victoria had made a tactical error. She looked out the window at the dark landscape, wondering how to reopen the conversation. Ty divided his time between watching the road and watching her, thinking about how he was going to kiss her, and kiss her again, when they got home.

The tensions from dinner eased out of him, replaced by tension of a much more pleasant kind. He'd start with her mouth, the kissing of her, that was, and he'd work his way around to her neck. It had been a long time since he'd gotten to the point of kissing a woman's neck. He could hardly wait to open his mouth on her skin and taste her with his tongue, to hear her sigh in his ear as he cupped her breast and felt the weight and softness of her in his palm, to . . .

He shifted uncomfortably in his seat and shot her a guilty yet fascinated glance. He was powerfully attracted to Miss Victoria Willoughby. Powerfully attracted. He wanted to get her home and take her to bed.

When she looked up suddenly and caught him staring, he tried to alter his thoughts of guilty fascination to ones of friendly interest, but he didn't think he was successful. The first sweet edge of arousal had stirred in his loins. He wanted her, and he knew it was written all over his face.

Victoria changed her position, too, more than a little unnerved by the look she had intercepted. Whatever he was thinking had put a definite glimmer in his eye, a smoky, sensual gleam she was too wary to interpret. She had never broken off with anyone before, and her time for putting it off was running short. They were nearing the outskirts of Talbot.

"Amy seemed very interested in English culture," she said, bluffing her way into a new conversation. "I should have assured her that not everyone in the United Kingdom dresses the same way I do. English women have their own varied styles the same as Americans."

"I'm not sure Amy was as interested in English culture as much as she was just curious about you," he said, giving her a quick smile.

"Well, I'm hardly a good model for English fashion. Charles did most of our outfitting. He had an aunt who used to send clothing along for me. Good English woolens are known for wearing forever, and the Willoughby motto has always been 'Waste not, want not.' Though I've never been able to decide if Aunt Sarah liked brown, and that's why she had so much of it, or if she loathed brown, and that's why she sent so many brown clothes to me."

She glanced across the truck to see if he was warming up to the conversation. She hadn't meant to give him a history of her wardrobe, but she felt if she could keep the conversation going, she could somehow bring it around to her chosen subject of breaking off. Unfortunately, Ty didn't seem the least bit interested in clothing. The subject had struck him dumb, and if she wasn't mistaken, actually made him look slightly grim.

"Thank you again for the peaches," she said quickly, trying a new tack by referring to the jar of fruit Corey had brought to school for her on Monday. She'd already thanked Ty earlier in the evening, but she was running out of ideas. "They've been wonderful."

"Our neighbor lady is famous for her spiced peaches," Ty said, wondering why he cared so much that her rich old husband had dressed her in hand-me-downs. She certainly didn't seem put off by the idea, and she wore the clothes. "She cans them every fall, and if we're lucky, they last through Christmas."

"It was very generous of you to share them, and everything else you sent, the green beans, and apple sauce, and beets." Her stomach rumbled quietly, reminding her of her half-famished state.

"You're welcome."

"The tomato soup was very good too. Quite gourmet." The conversation was struggling desperately, possibly dying. She had run out of gratitude. There must be another subject some-where in her mind, she thought, if she could only find it.

"Corey isn't much for soup," he said. "But I know how hard it can be to cook for one person, or even two for that matter. Some days, trying to figure out what to cook for dinner is the hardest thing I do."

"Goodness, yes," she agreed, sensing the con-versation was finally gaining a life of its own. "I don't know how our cooks did it all those years. I find myself falling into a recipe rut, where I cook the same three things over and over until I can't face them anymore."

"Corey and I go round and round too. He could eat pizza four nights a week and hamburgers the other three. We eat a lot of beef, having the ranch and all, but I like mine as steak. At least you have to please only yourself."

"Not necessarily an advantage," she confessed on a wary note. "And there's still the cooking to do, even after you decide what to eat. I could have single-handedly supported a Chinese restaurant this semester."

"You like Chinese food?"

"I love it." The not-so-quiet emptiness of her stomach backed her up. Chinese food sounded like heaven and just as far away.

"No kidding?" Ty was on a roll, back in control, and he couldn't hide his satisfied grin.

"Well, I love the way Americans cook Chinese food. We were in New York once for about six months, and all we ate was Chinese food. Of course, when you're in China, it's not the same. It's actually quite different. Moose nose and bear paw aren't euphemisms, you know, and neither is bird's nest soup."

Ty hadn't known, but he didn't think Lacey had any moose noses or bear paws in her freezer.

What she did have was a talent for *dim sum* and a poker debt.

"We've having Chinese food tomorrow night, if you'd like to come," he said. He'd have to get down on his knees to get Lacey to cook for him on such short notice. On the other hand, she might welcome the opportunity. She was into him for about seventy dollars.

"Oh, I couldn't. It's a school night and—" They passed the Talbot grocery store, and Victoria braced herself to just come out and tell him she couldn't possibly see him again. "And I really must—"

"*Dim sum*," he interrupted. "Steamed dumplings, spring rolls, shrimp toast."

Shrimp toast. Her mouth watered.

"Well, I have lessons to prepare, you see, and—"

"Wontons, those little scallion cakes, lots of steamed dumplings, some of them fried after they've been steamed, shrimp balls."

"You can cook all those things?" she asked, her mind picturing every delectable, savory bite he was describing.

"I have a connection. Spicy chicken packages."

Victoria couldn't believe she was about to be seduced by her stomach against her better judgment, but that was exactly what was happening. *Dim sum*. Goodness, how long had it been?

"We always have this special apricot sauce for dipping. It's real good," he said.

She didn't doubt it. Tiny spring rolls dipped in apricot sauce, steamed dumplings. Her judgment wavered, quaked, then toppled over in sensual abandonment. An unsettling sense of déjà vu swept over her. She ignored it.

"I didn't have plans, really," she said, "except for doing some grading. I suppose . . . well, the papers can wait another day without harm." She would break off with him after the Chinese dinner. She promised. Right after wontons and steamed dumplings, she would assure him that she couldn't possibly see him again. After she'd taken her fill of tiny spring rolls dipped in apricot sauce, after she'd sunk her teeth into half a dozen scallion cakes and savored a goodly share of shrimp balls, after all that, she would tell him there could be no more of this dating stuff.

How incredibly mercenary.

Using a man for food—what depths she'd sunk to.

"Great." He stopped the truck, and Victoria realized with a start that they had arrived at her house, the end of their date, and the exact place of their last kiss. She wasn't ready.

She scooted toward her door, wishing she were strong enough to enjoy his thoroughly wonderful kisses without being so overtaken by them.

"It's been a very nice evening." She wished, too, that she had more experience at this sort of thing. What did people say at these awkward, tension-filled moments that didn't sound awkward and tension-filled?

"I had a good time too," he said, smiling easily, which conversely made her feel even less at ease.

"That's wonderful. I mean—well . . ." She didn't know what she meant.

"You could invite me in for a cup of coffee, and I could draw up a map to the ranch." The suggestion was made with a hopeful note in his voice.

"Oh, I couldn't," she said, her hand tightening on the door handle. She had already blown the big good-bye, and now even the little good-night good-bye was getting out of her control.

"You might get lost without it," he said, "unless you would like me to come into town to get you."

"No. I mean the coffee. I don't have any coffee."

"Oh" was all he said, intentionally throwing the ball back in her court. Victoria felt the social pressure to do the right thing mount and build and overwhelm her.

"Tea," she blurted out. "I have tea." She was using the man for *dim sum*. The least she could do was offer him tea.

"Great." His grin returned with all its teasing promise, and she felt the flames of the fire lick up the sides of her proverbial frying pan and scorch her toes.

How did she get into these messes? she wondered. She never used to get into messes. She never used to get into anything, least of all trouble.

But she'd never seen anything resemble trouble as perfectly as the man leaning against her kitchen door, watching her put together a tea tray. He had taken his hat off and dropped it in a chair in the living room, right after he'd shrugged out of his coat and dropped it on the same chair. The moves had been casual, graceful, utterly at home, and they had unnerved her beyond reason.

She wasn't used to having a man in the house, and she'd never had one in any house like Ty Garrett. His physical presence overwhelmed her even when she wasn't sneaking glances at him, which was quite often—though always with the utmost discretion. She told herself she was keeping an eye on him to make sure he kept in his place. Then she asked herself who she was trying to fool. The man was easy to look at, seductively easy. His body was like a magnet for her eyes and tinder for her imagination. A less mature woman might have been overly fascinated by all the possibilities inherent in such an intriguingly prime specimen of manhood. Victoria assured herself she was merely curious.

She sneaked another peek.

Broad shoulders and a chest she would never forget filled out a zigzag-striped cowboy shirt of blue, pink, black, and purple, with opalescent snaps. His jeans were new, black, and fitted to perfection on his long legs and what she could describe only as his middle area. He was wearing a big silver buckle that said ALL AROUND—SKYLINE STAMPEDE. There was also a date that would have put him in his college days, his name engraved beneath a pair of boots with spurs, and some fancy scrollwork. If she looked carefully, she saw, too, what seemed to be wild roses twining over the numerals, and under the buckle, of course, was that mesmerizing, narrow-hipped, denim-hugged middle area.

In her whole life she had been around very few

men built the way he was, and even fewer who wore jeans. Suddenly she felt deprived.

Ty felt warm, very warm, edging toward hot. Having Victoria look at his mouth was one thing. Having her memorize his belt buckle was another. He doubted if she realized what she was doing to him, but he was pretty sure she was going to realize it in a minute if she didn't stop. He could have moved, and maybe that would have been the smart thing to do. But watching her stare at him was a seduction all its own, and it was over much too soon.

With a startled motion she went back to arranging her tea tray, breaking the tantalizing connection, but not breaking the mood. He wondered what his chances were of getting invited to spend the night.

Victoria nervously wet her lips and tucked up a loose strand of her hair, wondering what had gotten into her. Her appetite had fled. Her face was warm, and she had an unruly desire to look at him again, to move closer and touch him, and to quite possibly do other things as well.

Instead, she tucked up another loose auburn curl and rallied her composure. Taking a firm hold on the tray, she turned and forced herself to face him with only polite thoughts.

"Shall we have our tea in the living room?"

"Sounds good." He pushed off the door frame and took the tray from her, smiling in a way that riveted her gaze to his mouth and deepened her blush. A week ago he'd kissed her, and she had the feeling he could very easily do it again . . . possibly over tea.

She led the way into the living room, dismayed and yet excited by her wayward thoughts. Ty Garrett was a bad influence of previously unsuspected proportions. She should no doubt forgo the Chinese dinner, retract her offer of tea, and ask him to leave. Those were the circumspect, sensible things to do.

Instead, she sat down on the couch and asked him how he liked his tea.

"Straight." He sat down next to her, close but not touching.

Victoria arranged her skirt closer to her body and reached for the teapot.

"The ranch is three miles east of town," he said.

"Yes." She turned her head and gave him a small smile. "You had mentioned that."

"Due east."

"I think you mentioned that also." She lifted the teapot.

"You just take the main street straight out of town. There's a big sign telling you when you get to the Sky Canyon Ranch. It says John and Sylvie Garrett, but I've been running it on my own now for about the last seven years, since before the folks passed away." His voice grew quieter as he spoke.

Her hand stilled, and she slowly lowered the teapot back down to the tray. He was definitely telling her something.

"There's a big gate with a double 'G' bar brand burned into it. You can't miss it."

She didn't doubt it.

"I'll send Corey down about five o'clock to help you with the gate."

"That's very thoughtful." Her own voice was a bare whisper. The map suggestion had been a ruse, and he was telling her, actually confessing, that the only thing he had really wanted was to get her alone inside her house, where any of her wildest ideas could happen. It was very forward of him, and it made her pulse race.

No man of such short acquaintance had ever confessed to wanting her for anything other than a study partner or a lab partner. She and Ty had nothing of the sort in common. Academics, she knew, was the last thing on his mind.

In a fit of nervous energy she finished pouring. The spout of the pot rattled against a china cup and a bit of tea splashed onto his saucer.

"Excuse me," she murmured, using an embroidered napkin to clean up the tiny mess. She picked up the teapot again and poured her own tea, splashing a bit on her saucer too.

"Goodness," she murmured again. Everything on the tray jiggled when she set the pot down. She grabbed for the cream pitcher, but succeeded only in making it spill more. "Excuse me."

She concentrated on reorganizing the tray, cleaning up tea and cream, dabbing and sopping, painfully aware of her increasing clumsiness—until a strong, warm hand covered hers.

SEVEN

Ty brought her hand to his mouth, turning it palm-up, and brushed his lips over her fingertips. The intimacy of the gesture alarmed and thrilled her. She most certainly should have pulled her hand away, but all her "shoulds" were made weak by the gentle yearning in his caress.

Capturing her gaze with his, he placed another kiss in her palm, then traced her lifeline with his tongue. Without a doubt it was the most amazingly erotic thing that had ever happened to her, and finally she did the sensible thing. She froze solid as an arctic waterfall in December.

Ty noticed, with no small amount of chagrin.

Letting out a deep sigh, he lowered his gaze to their hands and wrapped his fingers around hers.

"Do I frighten you?" he asked, keeping his voice quiet and carefully looking up at her.

"No. I don't think so. I don't think frighten is the word." Her own eyes were downcast, her movements agitated as she pulled her hand free.

"Maybe you don't like me? Is that it?"

"No, goodness, no. I like you, Mr. Garrett, possibly too much."

"I see," he said, though he didn't.

"Actually, I'm trying not to frighten *you*," she said, her voice full of hesitation. "I have . . . you see, a rather unsuspected . . . licentious nature."

Ty was about to reassure her of his courage in facing these kinds of situations, when her closing statement caught him completely off guard. She couldn't have surprised him more if she'd hit him with a two-by-four. He wondered if he needed to double-check the definition of *licentious*. She couldn't possibly mean what he thought she meant.

"Are you sure?" he asked, not knowing what he felt more strongly, intrigued or confused.

"Quite." She situated herself a little farther away from him on the couch. "I'm afraid it's been proven beyond doubt."

"By who?" He'd never met a licentious woman, but he would have staked the ranch that Victoria didn't fit the description.

With a sign of resignation Victoria realized it was best to tell him the whole sordid story. She had inadvertently stumbled upon the perfect way to bring their budding relationship to its necessary end. Truth be told, though, it lacked any of the decorum and grace she had wanted to instill in their good-bye. It most certainly would mean an end to his wonderful kisses and that amazing thing he'd done to her hand with his tongue. Goodness only knows where that bit of playfulness would have led.

"There was a young man at Oxford," she began, thoroughly discouraged by what she had to say. She picked up a pair of sterling silver sugar tongs and dropped two cubes into her teacup. "I met him shortly after Charles and I had married. He seemed a very nice sort."

For Ty, the mention of Charles made sense out of the confusion. He settled back into the couch, prepared to dislike her husband even more.

"His name was John Williams," she went on, "very solid background, good family, excellent student. He was there on scholarship." Victoria knew she was smoothing things over, but she didn't want Ty to think what had happened had been John's fault. Charles had made it clear who was to blame, and she'd never had reason to doubt Charles's wisdom. Later, John's faults had become quite apparent, but the beginning of the trouble had been of her own making.

"We met in study group," she continued, "then started going to the library together, helping each other with research and what not. There was an . . . attraction."

Ty got the feeling he was listening to some kind of confession, but he wasn't sure to what she was confessing. The last time he'd checked, being attracted to someone wasn't a sin. Of course, she had been married, and he had yet to hear the part about her licentious behavior.

"I thought I knew what was happening," she continued, "at least on my part, yet I did nothing to discourage the relationship. Friends my own age were so rare. I allowed myself to enjoy John's company. Charles, to his credit, realized I was becoming foolishly enamored of the boy, as he put it, and not just nurturing a friendship."

"How old was John?" Ty asked, trying to imagine the old man in the photograph lecturing Victoria on being foolish. The image was all too easy to conjure up.

"Young," she replied. "Twenty-four, four years older than me. He was quite handsome"—she slid Ty a glance from beneath her lashes—"not unlike yourself."

Ty had to fight back a grin at her admission, but he wasn't grinning about anything else. Twenty-four-year-old men were notorious for their hormones, and unlike Charles, Ty wasn't jumping at a chance to lay licentious blame at Victoria's feet, not on the basis of what he'd heard so far.

"One night we met at the library as usual, but inadvertently stayed much longer than we normally did. The room we were in was far removed from the rest of the library, and we were the only people there." She reached for her tea and took a sip. Color rose in her cheeks. "I can't even remember now what we were discussing, but it seemed terribly important at the time. I do recall that at one point we reached a deeper understanding of the problem at hand, and in that moment we reached for each other like comrades in arms." She cleared her throat, a tiny distressed sound, and took another sip of tea. "Things got rather out of hand after that."

Ty grinned. He couldn't help himself. He didn't know what horrific behavior was about to be confessed, but even if the two of them had ended up in the throes of passion on the library floor, he'd be the last to condemn her. Hell, by his figuring, she was a twenty-year-old woman married to a man who at that point had to have been in his late fifties—and Ty was giving Charles the benefit of the doubt on his age. Ty didn't sanction adultery, far from it, but he knew people weren't saints either.

Before he spoke, he willed the grin off his face, in case she looked up and thought he wasn't giving the subject the serious consideration it deserved.

"I understand all about things getting out of hand," he assured her, reminding her of his own previous confession.

"Of course you do," she murmured. The color in her cheeks deepened. "I don't mean to imply that our situations were similar. For one, I was a married woman, not an untried teenager. For another, things didn't get quite that out of hand."

"Linda wasn't all that untried." He added the information matter-of-factly, just to set the record straight.

"Oh."

The silence continued uncomfortably, until Ty reached his limit.

"So you're in the library with John, being comrades in arms, literally."

She took a breath. "We kissed. Nothing as . . . well, as intimate as the kiss you and I shared, but more than was appropriate. I was quite taken up with the whole thing, so much so that before I knew it, my dress was being unbuttoned and Charles was bellowing in the aisle."

"Shocking," Ty agreed, imagining Charles in full bellow. "But hardly licentious."

"It depends on a person's point of view, I'm sure."

Ty conceded the point with a nod.

"What happened afterward only made the matter worse. Quite unforgivable," she said.

"John wanted to marry you." It was a guess, but Ty thought it was a pretty good one.

"How did you know?" she asked, surprise evident in the lift of her delicate brows.

Ty thought about telling her the truth, that he hadn't even gotten close to one of her buttons and he was full of ideas, most of them much more shocking than anything she'd told him. But he didn't tell her that.

"It's a problem honorable men have when they feel they've compromised a woman. They want to marry her. Trust me on this one." He allowed himself a wry smile.

"But I was already married," she said, making the obvious point.

"Yeah, well, some guys might have thought Charles was too old for you. That Charles had taken advantage of his position as your teacher and as a colleague of your father's."

"He was brilliant, though. It was a privilege to study under him."

"You told me." *Brilliant, and old, and rich, and cheap.* He noticed she didn't mention it was a privilege to be married to the old coot.

"John's pursuit of me was the term's sole source of gossip," she said. "And of course the library incident became notorious and blown all out of proportion, though goodness knows how. There wasn't anyone else there. It was humiliating. I tried to reason with John about his marriage proposal, but he swore he was in love with me, which was impossible. One kiss hardly constitutes a basis for love."

Ty wasn't so sure. He'd gotten pretty emotionally involved just putting her coat on her. The kiss they'd shared had only intensified the feelings. Victoria Miranda Elizabeth Willoughby was enough to work on any man's emotions. Her innocence appealed to him, while her body enticed him. Her intelligence intrigued him, and her formality dared him to breach her defenses.

"Poor Charles felt hounded out of his alma mater," she continued. "We left before the end of the term, and arrangements had to be made for my degree. I had done most of the course work, but not all. Charles made them take my field experience into consideration, which was actually far beyond anything they required."

Charles had been running scared, Ty decided.

Some hot-blooded young man had wanted his wife, and the old man hadn't been at all sure he could hold on to her.

"A tough situation," he said.

"Scandalous," she agreed, pouring herself more tea. "Charles was most upset. Outraged, really. I thought he would never forgive or forget. I had dragged the Willoughby name through the dirt. It's a miracle my reputation wasn't ruined beyond redemption."

"Nobody's reputation gets ruined because of a kiss," Ty said, fighting to control his anger at her dead husband's vindictiveness. "Especially if, as you say, the kiss wasn't even as involved as the one we shared after the dance."

"Not quite as . . . elaborate," she confirmed, busying herself with the tea tray. "But Charles's main reason for leaving Oxford was to spare my feelings. The constant reminders of my behavior created no small amount of stress on both of us."

Ty leaned forward and loosely clasped his hands between his knees, forcing himself to at least look relaxed. "I hate to contradict anything your brilliant husband had to say, but I don't think you'd recognize licentious behavior if it fell out of the sky and landed on your front porch. I also don't think you're capable of instigating such behavior, certainly not in a public place. Though if you'd like to give it a try and prove me wrong, I'd be happy to cooperate."

Victoria gave him a shocked glance. She didn't think the retelling of her sullied past had scared him off a bit. Quite the contrary.

"You're not married now, Victoria," he went on. "Neither am I. And nobody is going to come bellowing down any aisles."

He was right, but that didn't make her feel safer. Quite the contrary.

"As a matter of fact," he said, "from what you've told me, if Charles had bellowed a bit less, the whole scandal would have been confined to three people in a deserted library. Unless you're the one who talked about it all over the place."

"Never!" she gasped. "Not a word!"

"John wanted to marry you, and he was a friend. So he probably wasn't inclined to go around and ruin your reputation."

"He seemed a solid sort," she admitted after a moment's consideration. "Other than his infatuation with me, of course."

"Charles was the only one with anything to gain by making a lot of noise out of one kiss and maybe a button or two," Ty concluded.

"Oh, no. He had nothing to gain. We had to leave Oxford, for goodness sake. He was as humiliated as I was by the incident."

"No," Ty said, shaking his head. "He was a lot more than humiliated. He was scared, and he knew the best way to keep you was through guilt. The more the merrier."

"I can't imagine that," she insisted. "I did feel terribly guilty, but I was . . . well, *guilty*."

"Of a kiss. That's not much to be guilty about."

"It wasn't just the kiss." She hesitated, reaching for her teacup, then changing her mind and folding her hands back in her lap. "It was . . . you see . . . how much I enjoyed it, and believe me, it was nothing compared to how much I enjoyed yours, and that seems to be the problem."

Of course it was, Ty thought. That was always his problem: Women enjoying his kisses so much, they didn't want anything to do with him. Maybe Corey had been right. Maybe he didn't get out enough to know how the game was played anymore.

Victoria dreaded having to explain further, but one look at Ty's face told her he had no idea what she was talking about. She wasn't exactly sure herself; she'd never tried to put her feelings into words. There had never been an occasion when she'd needed to put them into words. She had avoided men for that very reason—the turmoil they created.

"It didn't seem fair to Charles," she said bluntly,

forcing herself to meet Ty's eyes and promising herself she would never date another man, if only to save herself the embarrassment of this sort of explanation.

"Charles is dead."

"Yes. And I decided not to become involved that way with a man ever again."

"You mean kissing?" he asked. "Or do you mean marriage? Or do you mean something else?"

"Well, marriage is definitely out," she said. "Definitely out. And kissing leads to all sorts of things that I'd really rather not discuss, but which I am sure you are aware of."

"I think I remember a few possibilities," he said, still mightily confused.

"Yes, well, you see, it wasn't so terribly disappointing with Charles. I mean, it was quite obvious his passions lay more with academia than with . . . with . . ."

"Sex?" Ty suggested, helping her out. He was still confused, but he was getting damned intrigued again.

"Yes." She drew herself up and fingered the collar of her awful yellow blouse. She had stopped meeting his gaze some sentences back. "But with a man like yourself, for instance—whom I knew right from the start to avoid, but with whom I still find myself somewhat involved—well, with a man like you the . . . uh, expectations, I'm sure, are bound to become unrealistic. I'm not sure exactly why. But even with my extensive reading on the subject, I find myself imagining all sorts of things. Thoroughly romanticized, I assure you."

Extensive reading? He was thoroughly intrigued. "Maybe Charles wasn't doing it right."

She cast him a prim glance. "Charles was brilliant, and according to my research, he was proficient in the basic moves."

Ty was beginning to get the picture. Charles had convinced her she was licentious because she had enjoyed another man's kisses, and to appease him, she had convinced herself she was frigid. An interesting combination. Sex, he knew, was confusing for a lot of people, but by his figuring, Victoria was more confused than most.

"I'm sure you see now why we shouldn't attempt continuing a relationship on our current course," she said, managing to keep busy by arranging and rearranging the tea tray.

"Not exactly," he admitted. "I haven't read any books or anything, but I know enough to know that 'proficiency in basic moves' doesn't sound like much fun in bed."

Fun? A cup and saucer clattered to the floor and rolled across a corner of the rug. The cream pitcher almost followed in the wake of Victoria's ill-timed lunge.

Fun! Her fingers grappled with the pitcher. She stuck her foot out to keep the teacup from rolling and spilling across more of the rug. One of her bobby pins slipped free and sent a loop of chestnut curls cascading down the side of her head.

When everything came to a stop, with her nearly spread-eagle over the tray, she stole a quick glance up at him. He was grinning.

"I guess fun wasn't in the books," he said, his grin spreading until his whole face was lit with teasing mischief.

"N-no. It wasn't." The man was unbelievable. Fun, indeed. What she'd done with Charles on the odd month had no more resemblance to fun than . . . than she didn't know what. Once or twice there had been a glimmer of passion, but more often than not there had been a sense of a duty performed, of comfort given, sometimes of a job well done. In truth, the faint rewards of sex had been less than compelling. Nothing at all like Ty Garrett's kisses, which had been very compelling.

He leaned forward and set the tray aright. "I can see where we're really on opposite sides of the fence on this thing."

Thank goodness, she thought. He had finally understood her.

"But judging from what you've told me," he continued, "I've had more experience in this area than you. That would make me the expert, and I think you need to give sex another chance."

Her face flamed. He hadn't understood her at all, not her motives, at least, though he seemed to have understood her goal quite clearly.

He went on. "I don't think a young woman like yourself should deny herself the support and comfort and love of a husband and children solely because of a less-than-ideal first marriage."

"I—I have no intention," she stammered, "of denying, or anything. When, or if, the right man comes along, of course, I'll consider . . . alternatives . . . or something."

"Well, darlin'," he said, taking her hand in his, "I've been giving this a whole lot of thought, and I'm pretty sure I'm the right man . . . the best man . . . the only man."

EIGHT

Impossible.

The word was still running through Victoria's mind almost a full day later. Ty Garrett? A Colorado rancher? The right man for Victoria Miranda Elizabeth Willoughby?

Impossible.

She'd told him as much, yet she was going to his house for Chinese food. He'd repeated his invitation on his way out her door and had practically refused to leave until she'd accepted, assuring her they should at least remain friends. They seemed to get along well enough for friendship, he'd said. She had agreed, though she'd made her position on his other statement clear.

"Nothing in common," she muttered, jamming her feet into low blue heels. "Absolutely nothing in common."

Surprisingly, he'd accepted her one-word summation without an argument. That was preferable to the alternative, of course, but she would have thought that if he really believed he was the right man for her, he would have been able to support his idea with a fact or two, an example of compatibility. One lousy example shouldn't have been so hard to come up with. They were both human, after all.

She straightened and tugged her cream-colored silk jacket into place. Peacock-blue piping skimmed the curve of her waist at the bottom of the short jacket and framed her chin at the top of the mandarin collar. Blue and gold embroidery decorated the sarong-style cream-colored silk dress beneath the jacket. She knew the dress fit, because she had bought it herself in Shanghai. A Chinese dress to wear in China. Charles had thought the sentiment painfully adolescent, but she had been only eighteen when they'd gone to China the last time.

Charles had said the dress looked cheap. She had thought it was pretty and exotic. She still did. Charles had said take it back. She had taken it no farther than its box and packed it in one of her traveling trunks.

She squirmed in front of the mirror, tugging at the side seams. Maybe the dress was a tad tight through the bodice. She'd never actually worn it before, and it was possible she'd filled out since her teenage years—though she hadn't noticed any of her other clothes getting snug.

Chinese food. She stopped squirming. They both liked Chinese food, didn't they? They both liked spiced peaches. They both liked children. Ty had been great at the junior high dance, patient and compassionate with the awkward kids and firm with the rowdy ones. She hadn't known she liked children until she'd started teaching them. They were amazing, much more interesting than she'd thought.

They also had a common professional interest in the grassland. Different professions and different opinions, but a common interest. And what about those kisses? Had they been so forgettable for him that they hadn't even come to mind?

"Hmmph." She turned and checked the back of the dress in the mirror, smoothing it over her hips, though there was nary a wrinkle in sight.

A Chinese dress for eating Chinese food. She wasn't going to change. She wanted to wear the dress. It would add a certain ambience to the meal, a touch of culture. It was appropriate, she was sure, and it was much "sunnier" than anything else in her closet.

But it was a bit tight.

———❖——————❖———

Ty's jaw dropped the minute she got out of her car. Through the voluminous folds of her brown coat he saw slinky silk and female curves, the same curves he'd felt when they'd danced, beautiful curves in all the right places. He swore right then and there that if he ever got the chance, he was going to burn that darn coat and buy her something else.

Corey had ridden back from the gate with her, and he bounded up the porch steps.

"Hey, Dad. Guess what?"

Ty tore his gaze from Victoria to meet his son's excited face. "What?"

"Miss Willoughby's dress is real silk, all the way from China. She got it in Shanghai. Pretty cool, huh?"

Ty started to shake his head, then caught himself and nodded in agreement. He didn't want Corey getting any ideas, but Ty thought the dress was about as far from cool as a dress could get. It was about as hot as a dress could be and still be decent.

"Hi, Victoria," he said, coming down the steps to take her hand. He hadn't argued with her last night about her opinion on any future for the two of them because he'd needed time to think.

She had some crazy ideas he had to get around before he could get anywhere with her. Any thoughts he'd had of not getting anywhere with her at all had died their last death when he'd seen her dress. Women were too rare around Talbot to give up on one who wore silk dresses slit up the side. Silk dress or no, women like Victoria were too rare to give up on at all, in any way.

The gloves were off. It was time to let her know exactly what she did to him, and to try everything in his power to see if he could do the same things to her. After two practically disastrous dates, he was hooked.

He wrapped his hand around hers and pulled her close. "I missed you," he whispered, kissing her next to her ear and lingering longer than was necessary or polite.

Victoria barely noticed the impropriety. She was too busy trying to catch her breath.

"We saw each other just last evening," she managed to say when he lifted his head. She knew Americans were friendlier than most, and maybe being friends meant casual welcoming kisses. If that was so, then she needed to work on coming up with a casual response. The suddenly racing pulse and flood of warmth coursing down her body were not casual.

"I still missed you," he said. "Come on. I want

you to meet Lacey Kidder, the lady who canned the peaches and beans."

Lacey? He hadn't mentioned having other guests, and certainly not another female guest. Victoria let him take her coat at the front door while she tried to peer into the kitchen, where Corey was talking to somebody. She felt something beyond curiosity, something akin to jealousy, which made her feel something akin to ridiculous. Of her own free will she'd terminated any possible rights she might have acquired in that direction.

She and Ty were going to be friends. Friends met their friend's friends. She took a deep, calming breath and readied herself to meet Lacey.

Ty stopped breathing altogether, his gaze fixed on her bosom. If the dress gave up and split a seam somewhere, he wasn't going to be responsible for himself. It was amazing to him, but she seemed as unaware of the provocativeness of her Chinese dress as she'd been of the ugliness of her other clothes.

"Sixty-eight, sixty-nine, seventy. Chow's on! Come and get it!" The cry came from the kitchen.

Victoria glanced at Ty with a questioning look. "Is that ranching slang? A high numerical countdown to a meal?"

"No, honey." He chuckled. "That's just

Lacey counting off the *dim sum* and her poker debt. We negotiated down to a dollar a piece."

The information was cryptic and interesting, but not nearly as interesting as being called "honey." In her life, endearments had been rarer than friends her own age. First a kiss and then being called honey. Friendship with Ty Garrett was going to prove to be a rather intimate affair. Surprisingly, she wasn't put off by the possibility.

His home had a very lived-in look. Every piece of furniture appeared lovingly used and cared for, but worn. Not all of the upholstery matched, but neither was it discordant. The soft brown and gold plaid on the couch mixed with equally faded yellow-and-rust-colored flowers in one of the chairs. The rocker cushions were navy blue, as was a small throw rug situated in front of the hearth.

The house itself was in the ranch style, with everything on one floor. From the outside she'd thought it had a sprawling appearance. The inside confirmed her opinion. The rooms flowed into one another off either side of the main living area. The most intriguing room at the moment was the kitchen.

Ty led her there, holding her hand. She allowed the contact, realizing she would have to talk to him about it later. She couldn't recall having met anyone who liked to touch her so much. At the same time, she couldn't recall having met anyone whom she liked touching her so much. They obviously had a few problems to work out if they were going to remain friends.

In the kitchen pandemonium reigned. Food and packages and utensils were strewn over a work area three times the size of the counter in her rented house. The sink was full of dishes, and pots were bubbling and steaming on the stove. In the middle of all the chaos was an island of serenity, the kitchen table laden with platters of the delicately arranged and decorated *dim sum*. Four plates had been set out with chopsticks, and beside each plate were tiny serving dishes of Chinese hot mustard and what had to be the apricot sauce for dipping the spring rolls.

Victoria was intrigued by the smells wafting up from the table, as well as appreciative of all the work involved in creating such miniature masterpieces, but her attention was captured by the woman overseeing the feast. Of above-average height and a bit rounded, with a braided crown of gray and blond hair, she was most definitely elderly—past her sixties, Victoria supposed—yet there was a youthful gleam in her pale blue eyes, a very nonsedate pack of cigarettes in her breast pocket, an incongruous lace collar on her blue workshirt, a snappy crease in her faded and worn jeans, and big gold hoops in her ears.

"Hi," she said. "I'm Lacey Kidder, and you must be the Miss Willoughby I've been hearing so much about." Her voice was all business and gravelly, and she strode forward with a purposeful step and a jingle and a jangle. She took Victoria's hand and gave it a good shake.

"Call me Victoria, please." Victoria's gaze dropped to the woman's footwear and her eyes widened. She was sure she'd never had a Chinese meal prepared by someone wearing spurs on her boots. The West was possibly wilder than she'd thought.

"I don't usually wear spurs in the house," Lacey said, catching the direction of her look and slanting their host a wry, sidelong glance. "But Ty was in an all-fire hurry about this supper. Said it was real important. Said it had to be *dim sum*. Said he'd cancel a seventy-dollar poker debt if I would get my . . . uh, posterior over here right away. Sort of on the spur of the moment, you might say." A full-throated, husky chuckle followed the pun.

Seventy pieces of *dim sum* at a dollar a piece equaled a seventy-dollar poker debt. Without a doubt it was the most interesting dinner arrangement Victoria had ever been involved in.

"It smells lovely and looks divine," she said. Surveying the dinner table, she wondered exactly how someone in spurs had learned the fine art of making *dim sum*, complete with tiny decorations made out of vegetables.

"Well, lookin' good is fine as far as it goes, but let's get at it while it's hot." Lacey pulled out a chair and sat down, and everybody followed suit, with Ty holding Victoria's chair for her.

Corey noticed the gesture and grinned at Lacey. Lacey noticed and grinned at Ty, and as far as Victoria could tell, he ignored both of them.

"So tell me, Victoria, do you play poker?" Lacey asked as she picked out an array of food and placed the pieces on her plate. The table was small enough that they all could help themselves, and they did.

"No. I never have. My husband wasn't much for playing card games, or games of any sort, really." With a dexterity she was relieved she hadn't lost, Victoria picked up a scallion cake with her chopsticks and set it on her plate. Then she reached for a spring roll. "We did have a chess set, but Charles took chess far too seriously for me to categorize his interest as a game." She lifted a shrimp ball to her mouth.

"Charles was a brilliant scholar," Ty said. "He took everything seriously. He wasn't fun—"

Victoria choked on the shrimp ball and had to be patted on the back. Ty was very gentle as he continued.

"—wasn't fun the way you are, Lacey, and probably not as dangerous either. Are you okay?" he asked Victoria. When she nodded, he gave her a word of advice. "The shrimp toast has the same spices and don't ever play poker with Lacey."

"You play with her and have apparently done quite well," Victoria said when she could. For a moment she'd been sure he was going to reveal part of the previous evening's intimate conversation. She was relieved he had once again proved to be a gentleman above reproach.

"We kept it penny ante until I was twenty-one," he said, "and by then I was on to all her tricks. The seventy dollars was a stroke of luck, double or nothing on a cut of the cards."

"Don't listen to him, Victoria," Lacey said. "We girls could stick together and end up owning this ranch, lock, stock, and barrel."

Corey giggled into his plate and used his fingers to snatch a wonton off a platter. Lacey bopped him with her chopsticks, but he only grinned and popped the morsel into his mouth.

"I have to say you're doing a fine job with this boy," the older woman continued. "He tells me you've got him doing extra mathematics and writing to keep his science up to snuff."

It was a subject dear to Victoria's heart. "I believe all the disciplines are dependent upon one another. I'm trying to work with the other teachers to coordinate our subject matter and curriculum. My father never gave me a lesson that didn't include writing. He always wanted reports. He was quite strict about his requirements for a completed assignment, but I know the extra hours of composition helped me greatly when I went on to college, and later when I started writing grants."

"Sounds like a schoolteacher all right," the older woman said in an approving tone. "What about your mother? What did she teach you?"

"Nothing of a purely practical nature. She died when I was young."

"Can you cook?" Lacey asked.

"In a manner of speaking." Faced with Lacey's culinary wonders, it was as much skill as Victoria dared to claim.

"Never had children myself, but I was married once." Lacey reached for another dumpling. "Then you take Ty here, who kind of got the cart before the horse. I've been thinking lately that he could use a wife. What do you think?"

Ty thought Lacey's bluntness was getting out of hand.

Victoria didn't know what to think.

"Marriage is a complicated relationship," she said, attempting diplomacy. "Certainly not one to take lightly."

"Walter and I took it quite lightly, dear, and remained gloriously in love until he died in the war. Young people today tippy-toe around it too much, trying to see if they're compatible, testing the waters long after they've used all the water up, if you know what I mean."

Victoria was quite sure she didn't know what Lacey meant.

Ty knew, but he didn't think an explanation was in order.

"Dad can cook real good," Corey piped up. "And he's got lots of water rights. Enough to run this place and keep hay in the south pasture."

"It's a nice spread," Lacey added with a chuckle. "Not too far from town. What town there is, anyway. But a woman can get used to simpler comforts. Corey tells me you've been doing research on the prairie."

"Grasslands are my area of interest," Victoria said, beginning to understand where the conversation was heading.

"Well, then, you'd fit in real well now, wouldn't you."

It wasn't a question, and Victoria didn't answer. An hour later, the only thing Lacey didn't know about her was her shoe size. Ty had headed off some of the more personal questions, but by the end of the meal Victoria felt thoroughly interviewed. Even more surprising, she felt as if she'd passed with flying colors. It was a shame she wasn't looking for the job.

A damn shame, she thought. She liked Ty's friends, she liked his son, and she liked him a lot. And those kisses of his, they made her feel alive. Her biggest regret of the previous evening was that she'd managed to talk and talk until she'd talked herself out of ever receiving another of his elaborate kisses. She needed to get her priorities straight. She really did.

"Corey is going to ride home with me and look at that new batch of pups," Lacey said as she tossed down her napkin and stood up. "I don't think we mentioned anything about cleanup in the deal."

"I'll handle the cleanup," Ty said. "You did a great job on the meal, Lacey. Thanks for coming over on such short notice."

"My pleasure. I'd be happy to do it again if another special occasion should arise," she said, a not-so-subtle twinkle in her eye. "It was nice meeting you, Victoria."

"Nice meeting you too, Lacey. The dinner was wonderful."

In short order, Lacey and Corey had saddled up and literally ridden off into the sunset, Lacey's place being a half mile to the west of the Sky Canyon Ranch. That left Ty and Victoria very much alone on the front porch and, as the seconds ticked by in silence, very much aware of each other.

Victoria cleared her throat and fiddled with the placket on her jacket.

Ty stood by her side and casually slipped his arm around her waist.

Corey turned in the saddle and waved, and the two of them waved back. The seconds ticked by.

"It was a lovely dinner," Victoria murmured into the silence.

"So is your dress lovely," he said. "I didn't get a chance to tell you earlier." The silk was soft and supple under his hand, the curve of her waist enticing, fitted to his palm with perfection. He took a deep breath and looked down at her.

In the next second she looked up and met his gaze, her lips softly parted, and he was lost.

NINE

Ty lowered his head and angled his mouth over hers, tightening his hold on her waist and pulling her into his arms at the same time. His other hand slid up a smooth expanse of curve-hugging silk, over her hip and up the side of her dress until her breast was in his palm. He groaned into her mouth and crushed her against him.

Victoria felt a moment's shock, then a glorious sense of reprieve. She would have her kiss after all. But it was more than a kiss, and even in her inexperience she recognized the changing intensity of his desire when he touched her. His hand scorched her through the silk, the heat stealing her breath and her will. She had no chance to resist, to fortify herself against his need. His arms were around her, his passion consuming her.

Ty plundered and teased her mouth, knowing

he was treading dangerously close to the point of no return. But she was soft and yielding in his arms, taking every nuance of his kiss and returning it. Finally, he'd broken through her defenses. Finally, he was doing something right, and he wasn't about to stop. Not yet.

He slipped his hand back down her body, pressing her against him, allowing himself one breathtaking instant of grinding his hips against her. Pleasure shot through him with sizzling intensity, short-circuiting any connection between his brain and his groin and pulling his hips back to hers again and again until things were completely out of hand. He had her backed up against the house, half against the door, his mouth hot and wet and all over her, his hand sliding through the slit in her dress to caress her thigh.

Despite what Victoria had thought, passion was not an emotion much within her experience. She was overwhelmed, and if she had been able to think, she would have agreed with Ty that her previous indiscretion had been a light thing indeed.

Ty Garrett was no young man of twenty-four, and he was no old man. What he wanted, he took—because he was able to make her want to give. Whatever magic was possible between a man and a woman, he ignited within her. She ran her hand around his neck, feeling the strength in his jaw as he kissed her and kept on kissing her deeply, with a carnal tenderness unlike anything she had ever known.

Her response was uncontrollable. It flowed out of her naturally, in the ease with which she lifted herself deeper into his kiss, the sensual delight she took in living out her fantasies of tasting his mouth and feeling his teeth slide beneath her tongue. It was heavenly, the freedom and the desire. He was so strong and hard. He wanted her so much, and his wants worked upon her like an aphrodisiac of unfathomed potency.

She clung to him, needing more, and Ty was ready to give it to her. Everything. He'd been ready for a week and a half, ten long nights of dreaming of having her warm and willing, of having her ready to take all of him and be taken in turn.

"Excuse me, Dad, Miss Willoughby." A small form brushed by them.

Ty froze stiff.

"Don't mind me," Corey called over his shoulder as he went inside the house. "Lacey sent me back to get her coat."

Behind him, Ty heard the soft nickering of a horse. He looked down at Victoria and found her staring over his shoulder in disbelief. He was completely sympathetic with her expression. He couldn't believe it either, that they hadn't heard the horse and rider approaching. Ty was especially amazed because he knew Corey's favorite gear on a horse was a full-out gallop.

"You were wrong," she whispered, easing away from him.

"Wrong?" He didn't want her to go, but neither could he argue the point or plead his case with his son coming back any minute.

She straightened her little silk jacket without looking up at him. "I do recognize licentious behavior when it falls out of the sky and lands on a front porch. If you'll excuse me, I think I'll get my coat too."

"Victoria, I—" He reached for her, but Corey was already coming back out the door. He had to let her go.

"Sorry, Dad," his son said under his breath. "Lacey and I didn't think you'd get a signal quite so quick. She's gonna be madder'n a wet hen when I tell her."

"Corey, no. I don't want you—" He was talking to his son but watching Victoria, and she was already hauling her coat out of the closet.

"It's okay, Dad. Do you want me to stay at Lacey's tonight?"

That got Ty's attention. He swiveled around

to stare at his son. The facts of life were kind of hard to miss on a ranch, but Ty thought he was going to have to have a talk with Lacey.

"No, Corey. It's a school night and you have to—"

"Thank you for the dinner." Victoria rushed out the door, half in and half out of her big brown coat.

"Victoria, please wait." She was already down the steps and heading for her car. Ty turned to Corey. "Stay put."

He took off after her, his long strides enabling him to catch her before she got her car door shut.

"Victoria, please." He grabbed the top of the door and ducked down to talk to her. "Can't you stay awhile longer?"

He was pleading, almost on his knees, and he wished he had more experience to keep himself from looking like an idiot.

"I can't, really." She started the car and gave the engine some gas, warming it up.

He didn't understand.

"Maybe we should talk before you go running off." He was sure they should at least talk.

"No, I don't think so." She put the car in gear, and the door shifted under his hand.

He had a choice: He could let her go, or he could stay put and get dragged down the road.

Fortunately for his physical well-being, he had some pride left.

"I'll call you," he said, leaving the emotional doors open even as he closed the door on the car. He stepped back and watched her leave in a cloud of dust.

He'd scared her off, of that he had no doubt. He'd come on too strong, moved way too fast. He'd liked it though, liked it a lot. And she'd liked it too. A grin found its way onto his face. She'd liked it a lot.

Victoria was mortified. Corey had brought her another jar of Lacey's spiced peaches that morning, and it had taken every chin-lifting corpuscle in her body to accept it without dying a thousand deaths of pure embarrassment. His attitude toward her had remained completely normal, as if he hadn't caught her and his father in the most compromising clinch of her life.

She had spent hours the previous night going over every detail, trying to remember whose hands had been where and doing what. The whole episode had proven to be rather hazy except for the feelings. Those had been all too easy to remember, to conjure up and feel again.

She groaned and sank lower into her bathtub,

closing her eyes. She was thoroughly mixed up. She wanted him. She'd figured that much out without too much trouble. Sex and Ty Garrett were simultaneously the most seductive and the most bewildering combination she'd ever known.

How could she possibly be attracted to someone she had nothing in common with except liking children, various food products, wide open spaces, small towns, and the same people? Except for agreeing on the importance of education? Except for having the same basic inherent politeness? How could she like him so much?

She'd be the first to admit that what had happened on his front porch had nothing to do with politeness, but that had been as much her fault as his. Besides, she wasn't at all sure where politeness fitted in with sex. It was just one of the many things she now realized she didn't know about sex.

She sank a little deeper. Neither Charles nor her books had prepared her for the likes of Ty Garrett. How could she have remained so ill informed all these years? So naive? She had truly thought passion was for others, not for her, for it certainly had not been for her with Charles. Ty was another man, a different, virile, incredibly handsome, tall, rugged man. But was he the right man, as he'd said? She didn't know, and she didn't know how to go about finding out. She doubted if she'd find such an answer in the library.

Sighing heavily, she forced herself out of the bathtub. She had dinner to figure out and cook, and papers to grade. Self-recriminations, personal analysis, and rampant confusion would have to get in line for another audience later.

Ty stood on her front porch in the fading twilight, not at all sure what he thought he'd get out of coming to her house. The least he expected was a few minutes of her time. The most he hoped for was harder to admit. He would like to talk to her for a while, figure out where they'd gotten their signals crossed, then pick up where they'd left off with her in his arms.

He raised his hand to knock, but hesitated. Okay, he told himself, relax, think things through. The most he should expect was a chance to talk with her. She didn't know he'd been up half the previous night thinking about her, about how she'd melted against him, about how sweet and hot her mouth had been, about how she was driving him crazy. She didn't know any of that, and he didn't know whether or not he should tell her. Vulnerability was not his favorite emotional place.

Neither was loneliness, and he'd had a bellyful of loneliness. He didn't have the time or the inclination to run around on the weekends looking for a good time and a little company. He wanted it all: home, hearth, wife, family. He wanted it more than he'd ever wanted anything except Corey.

The realization startled him, and he stepped back from the door. Did he really think he had to wed her before he could bed her? His next question was even more startling. Did it matter? And his answer was the most startling of all. No.

She fascinated him physically and intellectually. Emotionally she was the biggest wall of confusion he'd ever run up against. He'd known a few women in his time, and none of them had ever had him calling in poker debts, giving away peaches as fast as he could get them out of the cellar, and stumbling all over himself, trying to make some time.

A gust of wind blew in from the north, chilling him beneath his flannel-lined jeans jacket. Snow began drifting from the cloud-filled gray sky. He shivered and felt the ache in his ribs low on his right side. One of the colts he was breaking had knocked him for a loop earlier in the day, thrown him when he'd least expected it. He'd been too busy thinking about Victoria instead of keeping his mind on his business.

He guessed that about summed up his problem—and the solution was just a couple of feet away behind a closed door. He raised his hand again and knocked.

Victoria got up from her chair, surprised by the unexpected interruption but grateful for the chance to escape the piles of papers stacked on the kitchen table. She needed a better system for evaluating her student's progress. Nightly homework accompanied by written reports was a grading nightmare. She was swamped, and had been since the beginning of the term.

Given the draftiness of her old house and the near nonexistence of her current social circle, she had invested in a number of sweatsuits, or, as she preferred to call them, jogging outfits, though she neither jogged nor, she hoped, sweated. She was wearing a white one emblazoned with the flag of Denmark, another bit of wardrobe rebellion. Charles had been angry with the Danes for as long as she'd known him, something to do with a Danish history professor and a theory dear to Charles's heart. He'd had any number of dear theories, not all of which had borne up under scrutiny. The Danish professor had apparently been quite a scrutinizer.

Idly thinking of Danes and theories didn't in any way prepare her for opening the door and finding Ty Garrett. At any other point in the last twenty-four hours, she most certainly would have been thinking of him and would probably have been less surprised. As it was, she could only stare at him and remind herself not to accidentally and ungraciously close the door in his face.

Actually, that would have been harder than she originally thought. He looked so good, she found herself standing in the doorway, getting dusted by snowflakes, drinking in the sight of him.

"May I come in?" He asked the question softly.

She nodded and held the door open even wider. When he was inside and the door was shut, she turned to face him. He wasn't nearly far enough away, so she took a deep breath and moseyed toward the couch to get some distance. A few feet was all she needed. In another unexpected move he followed her, and they both ended up getting all the way to the divan and sitting down. It wasn't what she had planned.

"I'm a little surprised to see you," she said with world-class understatement, maintaining her composure by an act of will. "I wasn't expecting visitors tonight." She hoped that explained the rather wild condition of her hair and the sweatsuit she was wearing. She wasn't overly vain, but she didn't like to look unkempt.

"I'm a little surprised to be here myself." He took his hat off, and she noticed his hair was damp, as if he'd just showered. The snow wasn't wet enough to have slicked back the dark strands, especially under a cowboy hat. Upon closer inspection she noted other signs of a recent shower: a smoothly shaved face, a fresh scent devoid of the smells of dust, cows, or horses. His blue shirt had a just-pressed look. His boots were polished, his jeans clean. He appeared to be a man on a mission.

"I didn't realize it was snowing," she said, her voice cracking the merest bit. She felt ridiculous having to resort to the oldest conversational cliché in the book, as if he'd driven all the way in from the ranch to talk about the weather with her.

"Just started." He leaned forward and set his hat on her living room table. "I don't suppose you've got any of that hot tea you like so much? What was it again?"

She and Lacey had talked about tea during lulls in the older woman's friendly but personal prying. "Ceylon pekoe," she said, rising from the couch. "Yes, I have some. It will take only a minute."

"That would be great." He stood up and followed her into the kitchen.

Victoria wished he hadn't come, wished he hadn't followed her into the kitchen, and wished just looking at him didn't make her want to either cry or throw herself into his arms.

"Looks like you've been working," he said.

She followed his gaze to the table piled high with papers. "I'm sure Corey will be the first to tell you I assign too much homework." A lump was growing in her throat, making it hard to speak. She really wished he'd stayed away long enough for her to get her bearings. It wasn't fair, the ease with which he turned her life upside down.

"He doesn't mind," Ty said. "Not when it's for you. I think you're about his favorite teacher of all time."

"I can't imagine why," she said, hiding her blush by busying herself with putting water on to boil. "Especially after last night, I don't know what he must be thinking."

There, she thought, the awful truth of her brazen behavior was out. She'd shocked herself on his front porch. She couldn't imagine that she hadn't shocked him too.

The sound of his laughter brought her head around.

"He thinks you gave me a signal," he said, taking a step closer. His grin was a little crooked, maybe a little unsure. "I guess I thought you gave me a signal too."

She didn't pretend to misunderstand. She knew exactly what he was talking about. There had been, in her estimation, enough signals ricocheting around the two of them last night to light up half the town of Talbot.

"I think I gave you a lot of signals," she admitted, turning the water faucet off and setting the teakettle on the stove.

"I want you to know I talked to him, and he thinks we were kissing."

She could feel him moving closer, feel the warmth of his presence filling the empty space behind her. "We *were* kissing," she said in an embarrassed whisper.

"Yeah, but five more minutes of kissing like that and we would have been making love."

Honesty kept her from disagreeing with him, and propriety kept her from admitting to the truth, which left the silence for him to fill.

"I still want to," he said, and she felt his hand on her shoulder, turning her around. "I still want to make love to you. It's what I've wanted since I picked you up that first night and got you all tangled up in my coat."

The silence returned, charged and awkward and veritably alive with signals. He rubbed his thumb across her cheek and tucked a straying curl behind her ear. His touch was gentle, hesitant.

"It's not something I'm used to very much," she said, not knowing if she was admitting something or explaining something. She couldn't quite bring herself to meet his gaze. She stared at the buttons on his shirt, instead, and tried not to remember how wonderful it had felt to be wrapped in the warmth and strength of his arms.

"I know you've been alone for a long time."

She shook her head. "It's more than that. Charles and I, we didn't . . . we weren't . . . intimate very often. His health wasn't good, and he had his work. Sometimes I wondered why he married me. He didn't seem to find me attractive in a conjugal way."

"Why did you marry him?" Ty asked what he thought was the more pertinent question.

"He was—"

"Brilliant," he interrupted dryly.

"Well, yes," she said, not realizing she'd missed the humor in his voice. "But he was also familiar. The most, maybe the only familiar person in my life after my father died. Moving from place to place and country to country all the time can be very educational, but it can also leave you very unconnected to anything or anybody. Charles was my connection. There was love, even if there wasn't passion. If he was strict and demanding, he was also reliable and caring. I was happy to marry him. Not marrying him would have meant losing him, and I couldn't have afforded to lose him."

Ty slid his hand to the nape of her neck and ran the tips of his fingers through the straying ends of her upswept curls. He didn't know what to do with her. He only knew that he wanted her.

"I'm so connected to this place, I guess it's hard for me to understand," he said. "But if those are the things you're looking for in a man, I'm as reliable as the day is long, and I know how to take care of what's mine. I'm kind of strict with Corey, because I think it's good for him, but I'm probably not the best judge of how demanding I am."

He bent his head and placed a soft kiss on her cheek because he couldn't resist. For the same reason he kissed her brow, his hands sliding down to her waist and pulling her closer.

"I'm not sure I know exactly what love is," he continued quietly. "But I know I'm not afraid of it, or of commitment. Passion I'm pretty sure of. I seem to have a whole lot of it built up inside, and there's nothing I'd like better than to share all of it with you." He bent his head farther and brushed his mouth across her ear. "I *ache* for you, Victoria."

His whispered words and tender caresses made her tremble within his embrace. Victoria tilted her head back to meet his gaze and found her mouth covered in a searing kiss. She parted her lips, surrendering to the power and the beauty of the passion he was so eager to share.

It wasn't what she'd expected, to be tumbled head over heels so quickly again, and as much as she liked it, as much as she liked him, she wasn't at all prepared for the consequences of continuing. Making love with Ty Garrett was bound to be . . . *extraordinary*.

She sighed as his tongue invaded her mouth, searching and teasing. The muscles in his arms flexed and drew her nearer, crushing her to his chest. The way he kissed was a luxury beyond compare. It was sweetness and seduction intertwined. It was wonderful. It was dangerous. It was addicting. It was getting out of control.

"Ty?" she murmured against his mouth, trying to slow things down. "Ty?"

"Hmm?" His lips roamed over her face, stealing kisses and taking gentle bites until she could hardly breathe. No one had ever given such a good impression of actually wanting to devour her, to use her up, to taste her and feel her, to know her, everything about her.

"I'm not ready for this." The words sounded juvenile and stupid—and true. She was in over her head and probably overly capable of making a fool of herself before, during, and after sex.

"Not ready?" Ty asked roughly, his mouth coming to a halt on the tender skin below her ear.

He was ready. He was more than ready. He was ready for anything, everything.

"We hardly know each other," she said, her voice muffled into the crook of his neck.

Wasn't that what they were doing? he wondered. Getting to know each other? If he could just get them both out of their clothes, he had no doubt they'd know each other a whole lot better in very short order.

"Maybe you should go," she said.

Go? As in out the door into the snow? In his current condition? He wasn't even sure he could walk to the door without hurting himself. Didn't she know that?

Probably not. He groaned in frustration. Book learning was no replacement for experience, and from what she'd told him, she'd probably never felt anything like what he was pressing up against her.

He had to slow down, put his needs aside, and

figure out how to bring her around to his way of thinking. He was a grown man. He should be able to do that without expiring of sexual deprivation in the meantime.

"Can we compromise?" he asked.

"Compromise?" She sounded unsure.

"Yes, compromise. You're right. We don't know each other very well." He didn't really agree with her on that point, but he was negotiating for special rights and privileges. Tact couldn't hurt his chances. "Thanksgiving is coming up next week, and I'd like you to come out and spend your vacation at the ranch. It'll just be Corey and me, and Lacey. We'd all love to have you share our dinner and be our guest for the weekend."

When she didn't answer, he pushed a little harder.

"I like you, Victoria. I like you a lot. I want to spend time with you, give you a chance to get to know me. But a ranch needs a rancher just about twenty-four hours a day, seven days a week, and that means I don't have much time for courting. Besides, it'll be awful lonely here in town all by yourself. We could have a great time together, and you'll be thoroughly chaperoned with Lacey and Corey there." He sounded like a school kid, and he hated it. He was sure she was going to turn him down. She'd gone very still in his arms while he'd said his piece.

"Okay," she mumbled against his shirt.

He stared down at the top of her head, wondering if he'd heard her correctly. "You could come out Wednesday evening," he suggested, trying to keep the excitement out of his voice. "That way you'd be there early enough to take part in the whole turkey thing, getting it in the oven and all. Lacey always makes quite a production out of it."

"School's out early on Wednesday." She was still pressed against his chest.

"Great. Come as early as you want." He wanted to shout at the moon. "We'll have steaks, kind of a farewell to beef before the turkey eating starts." Knowing she was coming for Thanksgiving made any physical frustration he was feeling a minor inconvenience. He was winning the war. He didn't understand how, but he was finally, definitely winning.

When he left, he kissed her once more at the door. Victoria waved him off as he drove away, and all the while she thought about courting. He'd said he was courting her, which absolutely precluded his thinking of her as a casual dalliance. She'd never been courted, unless John's rampant pursuit could have been called courting. She'd never been dallied with, either, but of the two she highly preferred courting.

She liked him. She liked him in ways she'd never even thought about with Charles or John. Ty was exciting, and wonderful, and it thrilled her when he wanted to be with her. She'd never experienced anything like what he made her feel, and she wondered if she was falling in love. She wondered if she dared, and she wondered if there was anything she could do about it if she decided she didn't dare.

Her life was changing on fundamental levels because of Ty Garrett. Suddenly the knowledge wasn't nearly as frightening as it had been before. Maybe he was the right man.

TEN

Maybe she was being completely irrational, Victoria thought a week later, letting herself get swept up by a handsome cowboy and his wild kisses. Her life wasn't supposed to be wildly romantic. She was Victoria Miranda Elizabeth Willoughby, a woman who'd tried marriage once and found it stifling, a scientist of small personal acclaim but of international standing within a carefully defined academic circle. She was the co-founder of the Willoughby Institute, and until Charles's children dissolved the trust, her name would remain on the stationery.

So what was she doing sitting in her car in front of the Sky Canyon Ranch homestead on Thanksgiving eve with a suitcase in the backseat?

Taking chances. The answer was obvious. She was taking a big chance with a near total stranger whom she might be falling in love with. But then, didn't all people start out as strangers? With only a powerful, irresistible attraction to pull them together and make them something more?

Of course they did. And if the truth were known, her attraction to Ty Garrett was very powerful and irresistible. He confused her, but she wanted him. With his kisses he had awakened needs in her she'd never known existed.

Would it be so terrible if just once in her life she did something the way other people did? If just once in her life she let nature take its course? Both her father and Charles had always emphasized the rare opportunities she'd been given, to travel, to study, to be in the hallowed company of themselves—to always be the youngest person in a fifty-mile radius, to be sheltered from sophomoric conceits, whims, and fancies, to never have to put up with silly adolescents her own age. It had been a mixed bargain at best. Would it be so terrible if just once she did something normal, if she just once gave herself a chance with a man her own age?

Probably not.

So here she was, trembling with excitement and nerves, about to embark upon a four-day expedition the likes of which she'd never known. There wouldn't be any ancient awe-inspiring buildings, no documents steeped in historical arcana, no quizzes afterward. There would be only Ty Garrett, his son, and the matchmaker, Lacey. There would be only Ty, and his kisses, and the way he made her feel. High adventure. Her first trip into the uncharted waters of the human heart. Her stomach knotted in anticipation.

Taking a deep breath, she forced herself out of the car, telling herself she was being ridiculous. Uncharted waters, indeed. As a mere child she'd crossed the Rub' al Khali, the Empty Quarter, on camelback. Before her fifteenth birthday she'd navigated portions of the Nile, the Amazon, the Mississippi, and the Yangtze. Good Lord, at seventeen she'd survived three back-to-back excruciatingly proper months at Lady Blackwood's School for Young Women. Four days with Ty Garrett could hardly compare to all that.

Could it?

If her first evening was any indication, Victoria knew she had sorely underestimated the thrills and excitement possible with the men of the Sky Canyon Ranch. They'd taken a ride before supper and watched the sunset gild the amber cliffs of the escarpment on the north end of the Garrett land. They'd spooked a golden eagle off its kill on the way back home and had watched with wonder and amazement as the huge bird had spread its wings and lifted off into the darkening prairie sky.

Dinner had been the promised steaks, though Victoria would have sworn hers was actually a roast. She had left most of it on the serving platter and suggested they use it for sandwiches for the next few days, or possibly the next few weeks. Ty had laughed and proceeded to eat not only his huge chunk of all-American beef, but hers as well. She was duly impressed, as she was with the pudding he served for dessert.

"Corey made it," Ty said with a note of pride in his voice. "It's real cooked pudding too, not that wet-and-shake stuff."

Victoria wasn't sure what wet-and-shake pudding was, but she was grateful Corey had advanced to the cooked kind. "It's very good, very chocolaty."

"I put extra in," Corey said. "The pudding comes in a box, but then I put in chocolate chips while it's cooking, a whole bunch, and I add a little extra milk, and then I stir it real well. It's kind of like a scientific experiment. Sometimes I get too many chips in, and sometimes too much milk, but we always eat it, no matter what it looks like."

"You could make a chart," Victoria suggested. "If you measured the chips and the milk and kept track of your measurements, you could eventually get perfect pudding every time. I could even give you extra credit at school."

"Hey, neat. Maybe we can make some more tomorrow and start our measuring."

"Certainly," Victoria said, and wondered if after four days of eating with the Garrett men, all of her clothes would fit as snugly as her Chinese dress.

"Corey, it's your night to do dishes, son." Ty pushed away from the table and reached out for Victoria's hand. "I'm going to take Miss Willoughby out to watch the sunset."

Corey's smile slipped off his face and he gave his father a distressed look. "The sun's already down, Dad." Behind the words were disappointment that his father could have made such an embarrassing blunder in front of the divine Miss Willoughby, his science teacher, a woman who knew all about sunsets and stars and planets, a woman who was bound to notice that the sun was already down.

Ty read the message in his son's eyes loud and clear. It was a constant source of amazement to him, Corey's lack of faith in his ability to woo and win Miss Willoughby.

"I'm sure we'll find something to look at while you do the dishes. You just stay hard at it, and when you're done you can put in one of those movies we brought home." He didn't know what else to say to reassure his son that he had everything firmly in hand. Probably nothing short of a wedding ring would do the trick.

He guided Victoria out onto the porch after bundling her into one of his jackets, a fleece-lined blue corduroy coat. He had deliberately avoided her brown coat, having decided it must have belonged to Charles's aunt Sarah.

The night sky was black and soft above them, filled with thousands of stars and a large, bright moon. Off to the west, the lights of Talbot emitted a hazy glow against the horizon.

"Your place is beautiful," Victoria said when they reached the end of the porch and stood looking out over the prairie grasses and the Sky Canyon outbuildings.

"The ranch is a little rundown in places, but we're trying to keep it up and improve it." He moved closer behind her and pointed over her shoulder. "See those two sheds over there on the right?"

She nodded.

"Next year Corey and I are going to tear them down and use the lumber to add on to the barn. We've already decided to use some of the money out of our next calf crop to get a tin roof, and by the year after we're going to paint the whole shebang, barn and house. Corey is in charge of picking the color. He wants something besides what he calls flaky white. Can't say as I blame him, though I'm not sure about the pumpkin color he's been looking at."

"Pumpkin is a—a nice, homey color," Victoria said haltingly, very aware of his breath blowing against her ear. The man turned her mind to mush. All she could think about was him kissing her. It could happen at any moment.

"I'm all for homey," he said after a long silence, his arm coming around her shoulders and giving her a squeeze.

Victoria couldn't help herself. She responded by looking up at him. After a moment of meeting his eyes he lowered his mouth to hers and kissed her—just the way she'd known he would. Moving into his arms, she welcomed his touch, amazed at how easily she'd become accustomed to his kisses and to being held by him. Every time they were close seemed more natural than the last, as if she'd finally found the one place she belonged—in Ty Garrett's arms. The thought was foolishly sentimental and romantic, not at all worthy of a scientist, especially a Willoughby scientist. But his mouth made her believe in things she never would have considered before.

Ty wanted only to kiss her. He didn't want things getting out of hand. He didn't want to push her for more than she was willing to give. Since she'd come to stay for the weekend, he was supremely confident of making her his. Whatever it took, sooner or later she would be his.

Victoria knew she would be his too. She'd known when she'd first decided to come, and she'd known every step and mile of the way to his house. But she didn't know how, or when, or where, other than she was pretty sure the actual physical act couldn't take place on a person's front porch. She was safe for the moment to enjoy herself.

Or so she thought until his hand slid beneath her coat, and she melted deeper into his arms. Suddenly anything seemed possible. He kissed her longingly, molding her to his body until she felt every hard plane and angle. It was incredible, the heat and hardness of him, the overwhelming strength and gentleness. His touch was reverent, but thoroughly skilled in finding the peaks of her breasts and arousing her.

She gasped and clung to him, and Ty cursed himself for starting something it was impossible to continue to a satisfying conclusion, not on his front porch with his son inside and the temperature dropping. So he teased her instead, not wanting her to forget how easily they struck flame out of tinder. He unbuttoned her blouse beneath the coat and unclasped her bra. All the while he kept kissing her, long, drugging kisses meant to teach her the rhythm of lovemaking. He played with her breasts and stroked her with his tongue until it dawned on him that she wanted him, really wanted him.

A slow, coiling tension wound through his body with the knowledge, bringing him to full arousal. She wasn't just kissing him anymore. The soft sounds she made in his mouth and the ripening of her body beneath his hands were more than signals. They were surrender.

He murmured her name and held her close, resting his cheek on her wild curls. He breathed deep to slow down the pounding of his heart even as the ache in his loins grew.

She was leaning into him for support, her hand clenched around the lapels of his coat, her breathing quick and shallow. Without meaning to, he lowered his head and kissed her again, and then again. Her mouth rose eagerly to his, and all he could think was that he couldn't possibly make love to her on the porch, and that there was no way to go inside to his bedroom or the guest room, not with Corey home. But he had to do something.

He broke the kiss and took her hand, heading for the barn. "Come on, honey."

He wasn't the only cowboy who knew how to make love in a barn, but he doubted if the thought had ever crossed Victoria Miranda Elizabeth Willoughby's mind. No matter. He wasn't giving her time enough to think about it. He just got her there, closed the door, and pulled her back into his arms.

Her first kiss was hot and sweet and willing, all the encouragement he needed to open the blue corduroy jacket and slide his palms over her breasts. The soft fullness of her in his hands was a sweetness beyond belief. He opened his mouth wider to deepen the kiss.

Victoria was drowning in sensation. She hadn't know what to expect with his kiss, but she hadn't expected this, to be taken by storm. His hands were everywhere, unfastening clothing and baring skin, then doing wonderful, startling things to the skin he uncovered. His mouth was on her breasts and her belly, and through it all he told her how beautiful she was, how much he wanted her.

She was trying desperately to maintain some sense of decorum, but it was impossible with her clothes falling off. Every time she tried for a bit of modesty, he did something to make modesty seem like madness. It was so much better, so very much better to let him touch and pleasure and shock her.

There was nothing furtive about Ty's love-making. He was bold and sure, and his caressing touch between her thighs made her sizzle and melt and want more. She pressed herself against his hand and wished only that she was naked so she could feel him better. In the next moment her wish was granted.

Ty had felt her response and the need behind it. He shrugged out of his coat and spread it on top of the bales of hay in the corner. Drawing her back to him, he began unbuckling the dainty leather belt holding up her gray slacks. Light from the full moon spilled through the one window in the barn and spread over her skin in a shimmer of silver.

"I feel like I've waited forever for you." He unbuttoned the top of her pants and kissed the corner of her mouth.

"It's been only two, no . . . maybe three weeks at the most, I'm sure. I'm pretty sure." Her voice was breathless and doubtful.

He lifted his head and looked at her. Her eyes were full of wariness and anticipation, a veritable war of conflicting emotions. He stopped himself from lowering her zipper and instead began tugging his shirttail out of his jeans. With little effort he snapped the shirt open from bottom to top.

"Making love with someone the first time can be a little awkward," he said, working his buckle free.

"Yes," she whispered, her gaze carefully holding his.

"Basically, it's one of those really simple and incredibly complicated things." He began unfastening his jeans.

"I see," she said, though she most certainly did not. Her voice was the barest of whispers and her eyes widened without ever leaving his.

"I've thought of about a hundred different ways I'd like to do it with you." With graceful ease he lifted each of his feet and pulled off his boots.

"Oh." It was the absolute most she could come up with as commentary.

"And one of the things I've thought about most is you touching me."

Not even a hushed "oh" could get past that astounding confession. She had a better than vague idea of what he meant, and it took everything she had not to lower her gaze and look her fill before doing what he asked.

"Come on, Victoria." He took a step closer and shucked his jeans. "Please." His whisper ended on her lips as he took her hand in his and placed it on his chest. "It's been a long time, and I want you so very badly."

Slowly their hands slid together down the satiny skin and hard muscle of his chest and belly until she closed her fingers around him and realized with utter certainty that she had gotten much more than she bargained for.

"Oh," she said softly. "Oh, my."

Suddenly much of her research and reading finally made sense. Ty Garrett was different, much different, from Charles. To begin with, he was sturdier, much sturdier, which she supposed would make possible any number of things she had once considered quite unlikely. But holding Ty made her appreciate for the first time the absolute correctness of the term "thrust," a word she had seriously used only in conjunction with rocketry. It certainly hadn't been apparent in her sex life with Charles.

There were other differences too, most notably size and temperature. Ty's whole body radiated heat, and the part of him she held was no exception.

"Oh, my," she whispered again in wonderment, unconsciously stroking him, measuring him, and in turn becoming intensely aroused. Touching him made her pleasure double back upon itself.

Ty was way past the "oh, my" stage. Her open blouse and coat were draped to the sides of her breasts, where they pressed against his chest. Unable to resist, he lowered his head and opened his mouth over her, sucking as he unfastened her slacks and shoved them over her hips to the floor.

He pushed her back on the makeshift bed of hay bales and coats, mesmerized by the growing boldness of her caresses, needing to press against her, to be inside her. When he did slip inside, she sighed his name and urged him onward, surprising him with the soft welcome of her body. She was made to be loved by him, and he loved her well, slowly and sweetly bringing her to climax so he could fill himself with her pleasure. His own release came in the midst of hers, melding them together and banishing all the lonely nights and unshared seasons.

"Are you cold?" he asked a few minutes later, still holding her in his arms, still pressing gentle kisses on her face. He stroked her hair back with the palm of his hand and kissed her mouth.

"A little." Her voice was shy, but her hands were bold in exploring the warm expanse of his chest. "That's the most incredible thing that ever happened to me. I didn't know making love could be so—so totally involving."

He kissed her again. "Can I come to your

room later, after Corey is asleep?" He hadn't gotten enough of her, not nearly enough.

"Yes," she whispered.

The rest of the evening was very proper, with the two of them watching with Corey the movie he'd chosen, an adventure saga crossing the galaxy and mixing up lives. The two of them were polite but distant, sitting on opposite ends of the couch. For her part, Victoria didn't trust herself to get within two feet of Ty without having to touch him. Even at three feet she was afraid she'd find a way to brush up against him somehow. Once brushed up close, she'd find a way to linger, and once lingering, find a way to caress, and so on, until she'd proved herself to be a total wanton.

It sounded wonderful.

She slanted him a look from across the couch, over the bowl of popcorn and yesterday's paper, and found him watching her with exactly the same ideas going through his mind. He checked his watch. She checked hers—and they waited through impending doom and certain disaster, through startling revelations and amazing stunts, until the quest was fulfilled, the planets were saved, and justice had been served. It had taken forever.

"I think it's time to hit the sack, son," Ty said to Corey. "We're going to have a big day tomorrow, getting all the chores done and helping Lacey."

"Sure, Dad," Corey said without a hint of protest, pushing himself out of the chair he'd been lounging in in every direction. "Can I get you guys some more popcorn?"

"No. We'll be fine."

"How about sodas? We've got plenty in the fridge."

"Victoria?" Ty asked, turning to her to see if she needed another soda.

"No, I'm fine," she assured both of them.

Ty turned back to his son and shrugged. "I guess we're okay."

Corey didn't look convinced, but he was backing out of the room. "Well, just so you know you guys don't have to go to bed just because I am."

Victoria blushed and turned to Ty. Ty held his own and kept looking at his son.

"Maybe we'll watch another movie," he said. "Miss Willoughby doesn't have a VCR at home, so there's a lot she hasn't seen."

"Great." Corey grinned from ear to ear. "That's just great."

ELEVEN

Ty turned to Victoria, a small grin teasing his mouth. "He'll be thirteen next month. I guess at that age, watching a movie together is about as official and romantic as a date can get." He moved closer with every word, setting aside the bowl of popcorn and letting the newspaper slide to the floor, until they were both on her side of the couch, taking up hardly any room at all. "I've got the rest of the Star Wars trilogy, a few Star Trek movies, and all of the Indiana Jones stuff. Corey tried to stick with either science fiction movies or movies about scientists. What do you think?"

She thought Ty Garrett was wonderful. She thought she'd never seen eyes so purely gray, or known anyone so incredibly, physically sensual. He fascinated her. The feelings he aroused and sated were mesmerizingly seductive. She wanted more of them. She wanted more of him. She thought she was in love.

"More of the star ones, I believe," she said. "The first star ones."

"Okay," he said. "Let me know when you see stars." He lowered his head and kissed her slowly and sweetly.

She did see stars, and she heard bells, and felt fireworks go off in explosions of sensation inside her body as well as out. When he lifted his head, she was dreamy with anticipation.

"The chaperoning isn't working out too well, is it?" she said.

"It's working out perfectly," he assured her between more kisses. "Corey will be asleep in half an hour, and Lacey won't be here until seven o'clock tomorrow morning."

"Perfect," she murmured in agreement.

He kissed her once more quickly, then stood up and walked over to the VCR to put in the new movie. On his way back to the couch, he pulled his shirt free of his jeans and snapped it open. Victoria's temperature rose.

"I don't want things to get out of hand or anything," he said, "but I don't want to waste half an hour of the weekend either, not when we've gotten off to such a good start. Not when we could spend it in some good old-fashioned necking."

He settled down next to her and drew her into his lap.

"Necking?" She knew what he was talking about, but it was something she'd never done. Goodness knows, though, she'd never done what they'd done in the barn either, and that had worked out amazingly well. It was astounding, really, how well it had all worked out.

"Yeah," he drawled, pulling her down closer. "That's where we kiss a lot, and touch a lot, but only in designated areas. Some places are off-limits, depending on whether we're at first base, or second base, or third base."

She'd been wrong. She had no idea what he was talking about.

"That's how we keep things from getting out of hand," he continued. "That and you keeping your clothes buttoned and zipped. If your clothes start coming off, nothing's going to keep me from coming on to you. Then we lose."

"Lose?"

"Or win." He grinned. "I guess it's all how you look at it."

"What are we talking about, exactly?" she asked, hoping she wasn't being too forward.

"Well, in those books you read, they probably didn't call it necking."

"I don't remember the term from my research, although it is familiar. It's something teenagers do in cars, isn't it?"

"Yes, and when adults do it in the privacy of their own homes, it's more technically referred to as foreplay. But since like those kids in the cars we're not supposed to go too far until Corey goes to sleep, I thought necking was the more quantitative word."

She laughed, finally understanding. "You've been reading too many science reports."

"Only the teacher's comments," he replied, his grin broadening.

She snuggled closer and traced his grin with her fingertips. The smile faded from his lips, and his eyes grew dark and serious.

"It's been a long time since I've had a woman to touch, and love, and make love with, and I've never had anybody do to me what you did to me in the barn."

"Did I do something wrong?" she asked, suddenly unsure. She pulled back, but he didn't let her get very far.

"No, honey. You did everything right. More right than I've ever had it before. Maybe that's a little scarier than I thought it would be."

Victoria knew what he meant. What had happened had been wonderful, more than wonderful, and if he was the expert and he was worried, she probably should be too. She'd sworn never to let another man rule her life, no matter how benign the rules and the ruler. But Ty had something she wanted, something she hadn't known existed until they'd made love. She wanted that magical, thrilling closeness they'd shared and the sweet aftermath. She wanted it with him, and she wanted it more than was wise or prudent.

"How long until we can go to bed?" she asked.

He checked his watch. "Twenty minutes, give or take a few. Corey has had a big day, and excitement will usually wear kids out quicker than anything, even at his age."

"What about at your age?" A teasing glow lit her eyes, and his body quickened.

"At my age it's just the opposite. At my age it's the excitement that keeps you up all night."

"Good." She ran her hand up his chest. "Now, where are all these bases you were talking about?"

Thanksgiving dawned overcast and snowing, but by midday the sun had broken through the clouds and sent streamers of light into the Garrett kitchen. They glanced off pots and pans, shone on mounds of vegetables and spices, and glistened over the tops of freshly baked pumpkin and cherry pies.

Victoria had never taken part in so much organized chaos. Lacey had put her to work chopping, peeling, and reading recipes aloud over the din created by Corey as he set not only the fancy dinner table, but the kitchen table for breakfast, then did the cleanup after the first meal of the day.

Ty was noticeably absent between meals, but after lunch he coaxed her out of the house for another horseback ride, assuring her Corey and Lacey were old hands at putting together the Thanksgiving feast.

"We'll have to do all the dishes afterward, but at least this year I'll have help," he told her, holding her hand as they crossed the yard to the barn.

Victoria loved the feel of his large, leather-gloved hand encompassing her much smaller one. "From the looks of everything Lacey had going in the kitchen, we could be up all night cleaning up the mess." She laughed when she said it, but she also thought it was the truth. Lacey cooked with every spoon in the house.

He held her hand tighter and gave her a teasing grin. "That's okay. Staying up all night with you is getting to be my favorite pastime."

She colored slightly, but she didn't pull her hand away. His grin widened, and after a moment's embarrassed silence a smile of her own teased the corners of her lips. He was right, and he knew it. After only one night, staying up all night with him had already become her favorite pastime.

He had awakened her in the hour before dawn to make love to her one more time before he left for his own bed. The words he'd whispered of love and passion, of needs and pleasure, had been seared upon her heart. She'd lain in bed after he'd gone, wondering about what she'd done and where it could or would lead. She'd wondered about what kind of future they could have together, and she'd wondered if she'd completely lost her senses.

She glanced at the tall man walking by her side. For all her wondering, though, she'd come up with surprisingly few answers. Only that she was there with him, and if he kissed her, she would gladly surrender her senses again, time after time.

Ty needed no more invitation than the look in her eyes to lower his head and softly plunder her mouth. He would never get enough. Lord knows, he'd tried in the night. He'd held back at first, not wanting to offend her with something he might do. But as they had gotten to know each other's bodies, he'd pushed a little further into the realm of his sexual fantasies and found her open and willing, surprised sometimes, but eager to learn.

Then she'd whispered in his ear, and in one

fell swoop he had gained a new appreciation of library research. She may never have actually done anything beyond the "basic moves," but she had truly studied sex in a very scientific and comprehensive manner. It had all been amazing. He still couldn't believe his luck—going from years of near-perfect celibacy to finding a woman he was falling in love with who knew how to do things he'd never dreamed of.

He finished the kiss and ran his hands through the wild curls falling past her shoulders. She had the most delicious skin, and she'd left her hair free to frame her delicate face and wide brown eyes. Sunlight shot through it, bringing out the red highlights.

"You're beautiful, Victoria."

"So are you," she whispered shyly, looking up at him through her dark lashes, her glasses perched on her nose.

He had no idea what a man said to a comment like that, but it struck him like a bolt of lightning that he ought to ask her to be his wife while they were standing right there in front of the barn. His next thought was that he'd better slow down. He was sure of what he wanted, but he didn't want to scare her off. She had told him once how she felt about marriage. It was out of the question, she'd said. Of course, she'd said the same thing about kissing and sex, and they had certainly gotten well into the finer points of both those off-limit subjects.

Marriage was different, though. Marriage was a lifetime commitment, and she'd be committing to a rancher and a father. A man already committed to the land, a whole bunch of cows, and one special child. Any way you looked at it, it was a lot of commitment, a lot to ask of any woman.

Inside the barn he saddled their horses, his own bay gelding and a sorrel mare for Victoria. All the while he stole glances at her, watching her face come alive as she talked about the fun she'd had in the kitchen with his friend and his son. He watched her quick smiles come and go, and the seriously thoughtful look that came over her whenever she mentioned her work. She was beautiful, and he was in love, head over heels.

So watch your step, Ty, he told himself. No rushing her fences. He'd take his time, play it easy, and absolutely not ask her to marry him until Saturday night at the earliest. That gave him two more days to get her around to his way of thinking, two more days and two more nights.

With his arm around her shoulders he led the horses outside. "I thought we'd ride over to Lacey's. She's got a few things over at her place you might find interesting." He boosted her up onto the mare, then checked her stirrups and handed her the reins.

"The puppies?" she asked.

He chuckled. "Lacey always has a batch of puppies or kittens either here or on the way. But she's also got buffalo, about fifty of them." He swung himself up into the saddle.

"Lacey has a buffalo herd?" Victoria knew she shouldn't be so surprised. A woman who made *dim sum* wearing spurs could probably do anything.

"I don't know if fifty animals constitutes a herd of buffalo, but it's a passel of them. She and her partner supply meat to a few fancy restaurants in Denver and Boulder."

"The woman is amazing." Victoria gave her horse a kick to keep up with Ty.

"She is that," he agreed. "She sure helped us out when my folks died, taking care of Corey and all."

"How long ago was that?" she asked, concern softening her voice.

"About five years ago last spring. They were headed into Denver for something, got in a wreck on the highway. Killed both of them outright."

"I'm sorry."

He nodded in acknowledgment of her sympa-

thy. "It was tough on Corey and me, but it was probably easier on the two of them to go together like that. Lacey and my mom were good friends, so she just kind of took over for a while, until Corey and I could get our bearings."

They rode quietly for the next few minutes. The sunlight slowly faded, hidden by a low bank of gray clouds rolling in across the sky.

"It's been hard out here," he said, breaking the silence but keeping his gaze firmly on the western horizon. "Damn hard, trying to keep the ranch going. At first I didn't have much time or inclination for women. Then when I got the inclination, I still didn't have the time, until you showed up and I started making time any way I could."

Victoria turned in her saddle, fascinated by what he was saying. It sounded amazingly like a declaration.

He continued doggedly onward. "There's something about you, something really special. I knew it that night I first picked you up for the dance, and I guess I just wanted you to know that you're the first woman I've had out to stay with me and Corey. You're the first woman I ever made love to in my own house. Hell." He laughed self-consciously. "You're the first woman I've made love to in so long, I'm surprised I got it right."

It was all a bit after the fact, but Victoria didn't mind in the least.

"I think we got it quite right," she was surprised to hear herself say.

"We sure did." He looked over at her and grinned, then pulled his hat down lower on his forehead. He was the perfect American cowboy, a man of the West, riding easy in the saddle, his shoulders broad, his face youthfully handsome.

She wasn't sure she'd ever get used to that part, his youthfulness. She knew he was a few years older than herself, but anyone under fifty qualified as young in her book. Under forty was practically adolescent.

She loved looking at him, the same way she loved touching him. He had been a treasure to explore in the night. His body had been sensitive to her every caress. In his lean, hardened state, his responses had been easy to feel, and sense, and see.

Whether she dared or not, she had fallen in love.

For all her talk, Victoria had never actually seen a buffalo, let alone fifty of them on the loose. They were much bigger than she had thought, hairier and burlier. They were more seriousooking than cows too, with their huge heads, humped backs, and beady eyes.

"You get a few thousand of them, or a few hundred thousand, thundering across the plains," Ty said, "and they'll cut a swath bigger than half the Sky Canyon. The white man had to work pretty darn hard to kill them all off."

"So he could subjugate the Native Americans." Victoria quietly added her piece, watching the majestic beasts graze on the short prairie grass.

Ty nodded in agreement. "It would be like going into Denver and cleaning out all the grocery stores, emptying the shelves and locking the doors, calling off all shipments. People would start starving, and once the children started dying and the old people suffering, why, you could go in there and pretty much get the rest of them to do whatever you wanted. That was the whole plan, right here in Colorado. Kill off the buffalo methodically, completely, and starve the Indians out."

They sat on their horses in silence, watching the buffalo slowly eat their way toward a different patch of ground. An old bull, shaggier than all the rest, snorted and shook his head, sending up a cloud of gray dust.

"It would be amazing, wouldn't it?" Victoria said. "To see thousands and thousands of them trailing north into Wyoming, protected and free."

"Trampling fences and edging out the cattle, which is what people really want to eat, despite Lacey's fancy restaurant market." Ty swung his bay around, calmly giving her his opinion.

"I guess we'll have to agree to disagree on the Buffalo Commons idea," she said, fighting a smile. He'd spoken like a true rancher, like a man born and bred to the land and cattle.

"I'm all for agreeing on things," he said, a slow, easy smile spreading across his face. "Especially with you. Now, Lacey, she's more on your side to begin with, but only if she gets to own all those wild and free buffalo and can talk people into eating them three times a day."

Victoria laughed and turned her horse to head back home with him. "Where did she ever learn how to make *dim sum* like that? We had a Chinese cook once who couldn't make a steamed dumpling as tender as Lacey's."

"She and Walter traveled a lot before he died, and everywhere they went, they ate, and everything they ate, Lacey learned how to cook. She is the undisputed culinary queen of four counties. She's probably the only person I know who might have been as many places as you have."

Victoria gave him a surprised look. "Why didn't

she mention any of her travels the other night? When we were running down the itinerary of my life?"

Ty cleared his throat and rearranged his hat before answering. "Maybe she thought your travels were more interesting, or maybe she just thought you were more interesting."

"Well, that was terribly polite of her, but knowing we had something in common would have made me feel less like I was being interviewed to be your—" Victoria stopped herself in the nick of time, stunned by her own runaway mouth. She'd been about to say "your wife," and wouldn't that have been awful. "To be her employee or something."

Ty caught her hesitation, and he knew exactly which word she'd stumbled over. Wife. If she couldn't even say it, he didn't know how he'd get her to be one. Thankfully, he had time on his side. If Saturday felt like too soon, he could wait a week or even two. Then again, winter was getting ready to come on good, and he'd sure like to spend this one with Victoria at his side.

TWELVE

Friday and Saturday were wonderful days filled with sunset-watching and sunrise loving, horseback rides and ranching chores, stolen kisses and generous helpings of affection, and turkey-eating. Lacey made turkey benedict, turkey crepes, turkey sandwiches, turkey à la king, and turkey tetrazzini. She did not, the truth finally came out, believe in freezing turkey meat.

Despite the overdose of poultry, Victoria was having the time of her life. During her few quiet, private moments, she found herself wishing the holiday would never end. The Sky Canyon ranch and its people fit her like a family, with herself as the missing piece to make the picture whole. Corey needed a mother and Ty needed a wife. More important, she was beginning to realize that she needed them. Not all husbands were like Charles.

who though he hadn't been bad as husbands went, she supposed, had certainly given her no reason to miss the married state.

Unlike her years buried in scholastic endeavors, ranch life had an immediacy she found exhilarating, especially with a twelve-year-old boy on the premises, and a man who was equally energetic. After ten years of lifting teacups and tomes, she found watching father and son labor with hay bales, and cattle, and horses, and fence posts refreshing. Watching from deep in her lover's arms the sun come up across the prairie was as close to heaven as Victoria had ever been.

She didn't want it to end, and in her heart of hearts she knew Ty felt the same way.

Saturday afternoon was waning toward dusk by the time they finished up their last chores. Ty sent Corey inside to help Lacey with dinner. Victoria stayed with Ty, watching from the gate as he followed a paint gelding around the corral, swinging a loop of rope in lazy circles above his head. The loop picked up in speed and in the next instant floated over the horse's head, landing around its neck. Ty slowly approached the animal, talking in soothing tones and shortening the rope.

"Take it easy . . . easy, and we're gonna get

along just fine. We'll try a saddle on you first, see how you like it awhile. There's nothing tricky about saddles, boy. Come on over here and let's have a look at you." He stopped next to the horse and slipped a halter on the animal's head. Still talking softly, he led the horse partway around the corral and over to the fence, where he tied the rope to the rail next to Victoria.

"I'd say you're looking pretty good for being such a mean old cuss," he said to the horse.

Victoria silently agreed. The animal was beautiful, a creamy ivory color with markings in two shades of tan and dark brown spilled over its coat like its breed's namesake. Remarkably, the horse's mane and tail had the same colors running through them. The horse had been delivered on Friday by old man Harper, who was very unhappy with his latest acquisition. He'd traded a perfectly good pair of greyhound bitches for the Paint, he'd told Ty, and hadn't gotten so much as a blanket on the damn animal, let alone a saddle or his body. He had hired Ty as his last resort, though "hired" was too formal to describe a conversation that had revolved around Harper cussing about the "mean old cuss" of a horse he'd been gypped into trading his greyhounds for, and Ty saying that he wouldn't mind giving the horse a try. Money had eventually changed hands, sealing the deal.

"Maybe it's just Harper you don't want to take up with," Ty said, running his hand down the horse's sleek neck. "Can't say as I blame you for showing a little discrimination."

Victoria tried and failed to stifle a laugh. Ty had said as much to Harper, and after meeting the man, Victoria understood why Glen Frazer had made such an issue of Ty escorting her to the dance. If she'd had a dog, she wouldn't have let it get in Harper's truck either. His pickup redefined the word "rattletrap."

"The lady is laughing at us, Pistol," Ty said. "What do you think of that?"

The horse nickered and nudged his arm for another nose rubbing.

"Yeah," Ty said, feigning a conversation with the animal. "I'll agree she's pretty, but that's no reason to let her take us for a couple of fools."

He reached over to where he'd put a blanket on the fence and slowly lifted it onto Pistol's back. The horse shied away, but the rope kept him from getting very far.

"Whoa, boy," Ty said, running his hand over the horse's withers. "When they're pretty, the whole idea is to run after them, not away from them. I could teach you a few things on that score."

Pistol rolled his eyes and blew air through his nostrils, and Victoria laughed out loud.

Ty grinned and kept talking about the delights of chasing after pretty women, one in particular, until Victoria's cheeks were burning. He adjusted the blanket on Pistol's back and reached for the saddle hanging on the fence rail.

Victoria watched the horse shift his weight around and swish his tail. "You ought not to tell him such things, Ty," she admonished him.

"Why don't you talk to him, then? You can tell him I chased you all over the county until I finally caught you in the barn."

Victoria laughed again, despite her burning cheeks. "I can't tell him that. Why, he'd tell Harper, and the next thing we'd know, the whole town would be talking."

For the first time since he'd roped the horse, Ty was silent. He gave her a quick glance, then went back to busying himself with the saddle.

"They're going to be talking anyway," he said at last. "Not much happens in Talbot that folks don't know about."

He didn't sound too happy with the fact, which made Victoria uneasy—until he spoke again.

"You're a fine woman, Victoria, and I have very strong feelings for you, very strong. I wouldn't want to do anything to compromise you or your . . .

uh, reputation. Other than what I've already done, I mean," he added hastily. Then he went on even more hastily. "Not that I'd undo anything I've done. Having you here has been the best. Having you with me, just knowing you're here, gives me the kind of peace and satisfaction a man—any man—wants to have in his life, his home . . . his heart."

The last words were drowned out by Ty cinching the saddle and Pistol snorting. Victoria wasn't sure she'd heard them correctly, but if she had, *Western americanus cowboyius* was a far more romantic species than she'd imagined. He sounded like a man in love, like a man looking for forever and always—with her.

He turned to her then and took a step closer. She instinctively leaned farther over the gate, without a thought in her head except that he'd come very close to saying he loved her. The knowledge was new, unexpected in its effect. The thought of true love with him made her head spin, made her heart open. When he slid his hand around her nape and opened his mouth over hers, she tried to tell him with her kiss how she felt, how much he'd given her, how much she was willing to give to him.

Ty savored the sweetness of her response, reading into it all he wanted to hear. He'd come close, darn close, to asking her to be his wife, and she hadn't shied away. Horses and women, he thought. He'd heard other men brag that they had a way with both, but for himself, Ty had counted only on his skill with the bigger of the two. But look at him now. The mean old cuss, Pistol, was standing pretty as a piece of pie next to him with a saddle on his back, and the women he loved was melting in his arms like honey on a hot day. Life, he thought, was looking good.

By Saturday night they were finishing up the exploits of Indiana Jones, whom Victoria was hard-pressed to label a scientist, though she gave him good marks for derring-do. Films had not been high on Charles's list of preferred entertainments, but Victoria had discovered a real passion for them. She especially liked watching them with Ty and Corey. Lacey was hypnotized by the darn things, or so she said. Five minutes into the wildest adventure ever captured for the silver screen, she would be dozing off in her chair.

"Popcorn?" Corey asked, lifting the bowl toward the couch.

Ty and Victoria both grabbed a handful just as the phone rang.

"I'll get it." Corey jumped up and ran toward

the kitchen. "Don't miss this part, Miss Willoughby. It's the best, the part about the snakes."

There were a lot of snakes in the Indiana Jones movies, and a lot of myth and history. She had had wonderful discussions with Corey after the movies, doing what her father had always done for her with books—tying together information, sifting fact from fiction. She'd promised to show Corey pictures she had of Petra, the fictional resting place of the Holy Grail in the movie, but an actual ancient city in Jordan. She was excited to share with him the Arthurian legends at the heart of the movie and the actual archaeology work being done in Somerset, the possible site of Camelot. The Crusades tied in with the movie, which brought her around to Robin Hood, which apparently was another movie they could watch.

Education, history, science, literature. It was all so incredibly relevant to being alive on the planet, Victoria wondered how students could ever ask, "Why do we got to learn this?" She had never been allowed to question authority, and in this one respect, she was grateful.

"Dad?" Corey peeked around the corner, holding the phone and covering the receiver with his hand. "It's for you. It's Mr. Frazer, the principal."

Ty groaned and rolled off the couch.

"I just want you to know, Dad," Corey said, still holding tightly to the phone, "I'm pretty sure I didn't do anything." He hesitated, thinking for a second, then added, "Yeah, I'm pretty sure."

Ty tousled the boy's hair as he took the phone. "Glen? Ty here. What's up?"

Victoria's attention was thoroughly on the movie until she heard her name.

"Miss Willoughby? Yes, Victoria is here . . . Uh-huh . . . I see . . . Sure, just a minute." Ty turned to her, covering the phone. "Seems there's a man asking about you all over Talbot. Some people got kind of concerned when you weren't at home for a few days. Gossip must not be getting around quite as quick as it used to, or they'd have all known you were out here with us. The man's at Glen's house now, acting very official and like he knows your business."

"Who?" she asked, more curious than alarmed.

Ty lifted the phone back to his ear. "What's the man's name, Glen?" He waited a moment, then laughed, and laughed some more. When he'd gotten some of the chuckles out of his system, he wiped a corner of his eye and told her. "Jeremy Geoffrey-John James the Third."

Victoria sprang to her feet. "J.J. is in Talbot?"

Ty saw the surprise and the delight on her face, then the facts struck home. Jeremy

Geoffrey-John James the Third had been her personal secretary. Victoria had had a man as a secretary. He found the realization disconcerting and strange. He'd never met a male secretary. He didn't think he'd ever even heard of a male secretary.

Glen was talking to him again, and Ty forced his attention back to the principal. He didn't like what he heard about Mr. James insisting on seeing Victoria, and how if she would come home he would meet her at her house. Ty quickly put together the facts that it was well past sunset and the nearest hotel was over an hour and half away, and that considering the delight on Victoria's face, it wouldn't be at all out of the question for her to ask this Jeremy Geoffrey-John to spend the night at her house.

Ty was not jealous. He made that very clear to himself. He had no reason to be jealous. It was obvious Victoria was in love with him even if no words had been spoken. Besides, tonight was his night to propose, and he wasn't about to lose his chance because some ex-employee of hers happened to pop into town from who knows where for who knew why.

"Send him on out here, Glen. You know he can't get lost. We'll be happy to put him up, unless he's got someplace else he has to be."

No such luck. Ty hid his disappointment and kept listening to Glen Frazer.

"Sure . . . sure." He held the phone out for Victoria. "He'd like to talk with you."

Five minutes later Corey was straightening up the living room, Lacey and Victoria were changing the sheets on Ty's bed—Ty would bunk with Corey while J.J. took his bedroom—and Ty was wondering how in the world he was going to pull off a proposal in the middle of an invasion.

One person wasn't an invasion, of course, but more than a person was coming to the ranch. Jeremy Geoffrey-John James the Third would be bringing memories and the past. The noble past, Ty reminded himself. A past filled with wealth, servants, and world travels, with large estates in Kent and private secretaries. And hand-me-down clothes and boring brilliance.

He wasn't worried, he told himself. There was no reason to worry. Victoria had said she liked her new life better. She liked the independence, which she wouldn't lose by marrying him. He wanted an independent woman. As for her secretary, there was no real reason to worry about him. What could a male secretary possibly be like? The word "wimp" came to mind. J.J. James was probably underfed and half blind, meek and overwrought, balding and timid. He was probably coming to beg Victoria for help, maybe even money. He probably hadn't done very well for himself since he'd lost his job. Victoria, kind soul that she was, probably felt some responsibility for her ex-employee. Truth was, though, there was very little call for male secretaries in Talbot. The man would have to go elsewhere to find work.

Ty felt better once he'd thought things through, and he kept feeling better right up until J. J. James arrived. The secretary and Victoria shared a warm welcome at the front door while Ty, Corey, and Lacey looked on from the middle of the living room, where they had all congregated at the sound of knocking.

"Half blind" was the only thing Ty had guessed correctly. The man's glasses were noticeably thick. So was the hair on his head, thick and neatly cut, and of a shade to match Victoria's. He was most definitely not underfed. Athletic muscles gave his body an easy grace, and the classic clothes he wore defined that grace as elegance. As for meek, over-wrought, and timid, Ty quickly replaced those adjectives with arrogant, intelligent, and fearless—considering how close Ty was to demanding J.J. release Victoria from an overlong, overly affectionate hug, or suffer the consequences.

"Dad?" Corey nudged him with his elbow,

silently suggesting his father do something before J. J. James ran off with his science teacher.

"Yeah, Ty," Lacey said. She obviously agreed with Corey, but with an added need for haste in her tone, as if she were all too aware of the potential combustion point when a man and a woman were stuck together like that for too long.

Ty got both messages loud and clear and reacted with what he thought was appropriate action. He cleared his throat.

Corey let out a ragged sigh of disappointment and buried his face in his hands. Lacey snorted.

Ty didn't know what else to do. He loved Victoria, but she didn't belong to him. He had no right to tell her who she could and could not hug. He certainly didn't have any right to monitor the enthusiasm of her greetings. The best marriage he'd seen had been his parents', where two people had accepted each other for what they'd been, good points and bad, which to his way of thinking had often seemed like the same points.

If Victoria was happy to see her old secretary, who wasn't old at all, then he had to accept her happiness and not think it showed that he meant any less to her. Logic and reason, that was a man's way.

"Mr. James?" He stepped forward with his

hand out, very illogically and with only one reason. "I'm Ty Garrett."

The embrace ended in a second with introductions given all around amid handshakes and smiles. The smiles were short-lived, though.

"I've come to take her back," J.J. said after they were all seated in the living room, with coffee and cookies graciously served by Lacey. "The Willoughby Institute is struggling for its very life, and quite frankly, the board and I believe Victoria is the only one who can save it. We all know how wretched Neville can get, and he's quite out of hand. He wants all of Charles's assets going to Wickham. He'd like nothing better than to see the institute dismantled and done away with. His own father's life's work, if you can imagine."

Ty knew just enough about wretched Neville, Charles's eldest son, to easily imagine J.J.'s scenario. What he didn't know was how much of it still mattered to Victoria. He didn't have to wait long to find out.

"He has to be stopped," she said, her voice ringing with conviction. "The institute was Charles's gift to future generations. It was part of the prime directive. The last ten years of his life were dedicated to leaving behind a funded and staffed independent research facility capable of—oh, J.J." She suddenly reached out and touched her secretary's arm. "What about the Charles Edward Willoughby the Fourth scholarships? Did they get awarded this year?"

At the sad shake of J.J.'s head, Victoria withdrew her hand and fell silent for a moment. When she spoke, a hint of anger colored her words.

"To cut me off without a cent is one thing. I've learned to live quite comfortably. But I already have the best education money can buy, and for Neville to deprive the young men and women expecting their Charles Edward Willoughby the Fourth scholarships of their chance at the same education is untenable."

Ty had kept his silence, watching the atmosphere change from one of delight, to curiosity and concern, to fervent crusade. He noted the satisfied smile on J.J.'s face and the gleam of righteousness in Victoria's eye, and he put his foot right in the middle of it.

"Now, hold on here," he said. So help him, it was his night to propose, and he wasn't about to lose the proposee to some overly cultured, highbrowed male secretary. "Seems to me this whole thing is a lot more complicated than it looks. If the institute has a board of directors, shouldn't they be the ones to clear up the scholarship mess?"

"Under normal circumstances," J.J. said, and Victoria nodded. "But—"

"But I'm the co-founder of the institute," Victoria interrupted. "Charles and I worked on it together, and because my name is still Willoughby, it puts me in a unique public position that none of the other board members can take advantage of. Victoria Willoughby campaigning for the survival of the Willoughby Institute is far different from a group of unrelated men trying to save someone else's dream. I *am* the dream."

"You have a responsibility," J.J. chorused, and Ty liked him even less than when he'd been hugging Victoria at the door. As for the part about her name still being Willoughby, well, darn it, that was exactly the part he was trying to change.

"My name is on the charter," she continued, unknowingly reinforcing his point for him.

"You're the only one who can save the institute and the scholarships," J.J. reiterated. "Otherwise Neville will have it all. Neville and Wickham."

"Oh, dear," Victoria murmured.

Ty was getting the same feeling he'd had the night of the dance, when no matter how hard he'd tried, he hadn't been able to get a second dance with her. He had a lot more than a dance on the table tonight, and at least two other people in the room seemed to know it. Corey hadn't said a word, and Lacey was looking as suspicious as all get out.

"What's your stake in this?" the older woman asked J.J. with typical bluntness.

"My reputation, madam," he replied without hesitation. "I have been closely associated with the Willoughby Institute from its inception. To have it fail without doing everything within my power to save it would be a serious dereliction of duty."

"Not to mention the shortest road to the unemployment line," Lacey added with a shrewd glance.

J.J. had the decency to look offended. "Let me assure you, Ms. Kidder, my own welfare is in much less jeopardy than the institute's. Should Neville win, I will always be able to find adequate employment precisely because of the level of loyalty I am exhibiting in this instance. A secretary's loyalty is everything." He paused and turned toward Victoria. "Much like a wife's."

Charles is dead. Ty thought the words so strongly, at first he thought he'd said them aloud. When he realized he hadn't, he thought maybe he should, just to remind everybody. Charles was dead. Victoria had a new life.

He looked over at her. Her face was drawn and

serious. No doubt she was contemplating J.J.'s words.

"What do you suggest?" she asked her secretary.

J.J. was ready with an answer, and upon hearing it, Ty felt doomed.

"Come back to London. The board is willing to reinstate you and work with you to retain your bequest if you'll help them fight Neville. It's the only chance the Willoughby Institute has of surviving. Having the remaining founder out of the country doing menial, unrelated labor looks very bad to the courts. Neville is capitalizing on your current employment situation. If you had taken a position at a university, you would still be considered a viable entity. But, dear, teaching small children in the middle of nowhere is hardly doing *your* reputation any good."

Ty was definitely offended and tried hard not to look it. Talbot may not be London, but . . . well, there was no doubt about it. Talbot wasn't London, and seventh-graders weren't university students.

"They're rather nice, you know, small children," Victoria said, looking much like she had the night he'd first met her. Somewhat lost, somewhat overwhelmed.

"I know you, Victoria," J.J. said. "Loyalty and

responsibility are your first and second natures. You always do the right thing."

Silence descended on the living room like a dark, rain-filled cloud, weighing on everyone. Corey was the one who finally spoke.

"Are you leaving us, Miss Willoughby?"

Victoria looked up at J.J. "I have responsibilities here too."

"I would be the last to underestimate your worth to the Talbot school district," J.J. said, "but it is not going to fall apart and disappear without you. The institute very well might. The school district can easily replace you with another teacher. To the institute, you are irreplaceable."

Ty rose suddenly, having reached his limit. "Victoria, could I see you in the kitchen, please."

He heard Lacey breathe a sigh of relief, which he thought was misplaced. He didn't know what he was going to say, but, by God, he knew he had to say something or he was going to lose her. He took her hand when she stood up, and together they made their escape.

In the kitchen she immediately went into his arms, holding on to him as though she would never let him go. He stroked her back and cradled her head to his shoulder.

"Do you want me to ask him to leave, honey?" He knew he was taking a chance, offering to fight her battles for her, and he wasn't surprised when she turned him down with a shake of her head. He was saddened, but he wasn't surprised. He wanted to fight her battles, make her decisions, keep the world at bay. But he knew that that would be the quickest way to lose her, even quicker than doing what J.J. wanted.

"I have to go," she murmured against his chest.

"No, you don't," he said immediately, his voice as firm as his conviction. "They've been getting along without you this long, they can do it awhile longer."

"They can do it until it's all gone," she agreed, lifting her head to look at him. "I want better than that for the institute, especially for those students who have fought so hard for their scholarships. And I guess I want it for Charles too."

"Charles is dead." He wanted to say it about fourteen times, but he held himself to once.

"Not as long as the Willoughby Institute is doing his work."

All the more reason to let the damn thing go, Ty thought. Hell, it was his own son who wanted the money.

"Doesn't Neville have any rights in this?" he asked. "Shouldn't he be able to decide what happens to the institute?"

"You don't understand. It's more than the

institute and the scholarships. It's a wealth of knowledge Charles and I believed in. I still believe in it."

She was holding on to him, her head lying on his chest, but she was slipping away, miles and miles away. He felt it in every bone he had.

"I don't want you to go." His voice was gruff. He didn't dare get any plainer. She was a grown woman, and making love to her a few times didn't put his brand on her. If she stayed, it had to be because she wanted to stay.

"I have to go, Ty. I made commitments, promises."

Above all else, Ty knew she was a woman of her word. She'd made commitments in Talbot too, but the ones in London were older, stronger.

He'd lost. Way down in his heart he knew it. He held her as long as he could, and later that night he went to her room and made love with her one last time.

When morning came he watched her leave with Jeremy Geoffrey-John James III.

"Buck up, son," he said when Corey got to looking sad and abandoned.

"Maybe next time, son," Lacey said to the older Garrett, patting his arm as she passed him on her way back into the house. Corey followed her, leaving Ty alone on the front porch to watch a storm roll down out of Wyoming.

Winter was getting ready to come on good, all right. He sighed and stuck his hands in his coat pockets, still staring at the ranch road. She was gone, and she wouldn't be back. By his way of thinking, it had been a miracle that Victoria Miranda Elizabeth Willoughby had ever shown up in Talbot, Colorado, in the first place. Only a fool would bet on a miracle happening twice.

THIRTEEN

London was decked out in full regalia for the Christmas holidays, so romantic, so Dickensian, so incredibly lonely. It was snowing again, a wet, chilling, gray snow that no amount of baubles and tinsel could cover. Victoria sighed and forced her gaze back to her desk.

She tidied up a stack of C.E.W.IV stationery and reached for a C.E.W.IV pen out of an elaborate C.E.W.IV hand-carved mahogany pencil cup. She'd been wrong about the stationery. Her name wasn't on it. Her name wasn't on anything except page three of the Willoughby Institute directory. Page three. Apparently, Charles had overseen a few changes he'd forgotten to tell her about before his death.

She'd been in London for almost a month and was still working on saving the C.E.W.IV scholarships. Her modest bequest was at the bottom of the board's priority list, not having near the charm and cachet of a publicly given scholarship. Everyone was interested in her well-being and future, especially as long as she was working with them against Neville. But even she had to agree, they were sure, that working toward the whole Willoughby pie made more sense than trying to extract a thin sliver that benefited no one except herself. Actually, she did agree. She wasn't destitute, and she did feel the greater good came from saving the institute intact. At least that was how she'd felt in the beginning.

She came to work every morning, walking through the door of the Willoughby Institute and into an office marked C.E.W.IV. She spent all day with C.E.W.IV's portrait staring down at her, all sunken jowls and thinning hair, and she had decided that he had been a singularly unattractive man, thereby shocking herself into working harder to make up for such nonsensical thoughts. He'd been brilliant. He'd told her so himself a hundred thousand times. If she'd ever entertained a doubt, all she had to do was look at the four walls covered with awards, citations, degrees, commendations, et cetera, et cetera.

The room reminded her a lot of home. She'd always covered her walls with the tangible evidence of her intelligence too. It all looked rather silly now.

Charles had smoked, and on his desk was a C.E.W.IV ashtray with a book of C.E.W.IV matches, gold script on a hunter-green background. Willoughby colors.

Ty Garrett didn't smoke.

Victoria closed her eyes and rested her chin in the palm of her hand, leaning her elbow on the desk and dreamily slipping off into memories. Such slips of the mind happened at least twenty times a day, and she'd given up counting them at night.

Ty had the most dazzling white smile. His lips were so firm, his kiss so tender. She loved the way he tasted. She missed the way he felt. She missed him, and the more she missed him, the more she doubted the necessity of her presence in London.

She'd taken a leave of absence from her teaching job in Talbot. The school board had allowed it, but had held out no guarantees, given her lack of tenure or even longevity. She'd worked three months, then asked for three weeks off. Combined with her two weeks of Christmas vacation, she had hoped to have her work in London finished and be back in Colorado by January. Reality had hit her shortly after her arrival. Saving the Willoughby Institute was not a five-week job; it was a lifetime job.

A lifetime of shuffling C.E.W.IV papers and

folders. A lifetime of fighting Neville. A lifetime of initials and roman numerals. She didn't think she was quite up to it. She didn't think she was up to it at all.

She opened her eyes and lowered her gaze to the business at hand, the C.E.W.IV scholarship number three. What on earth, she wondered, made William Scott Fitzgerald's education more important than Corey Garrett's? William Scott was to be the third recipient of the coveted scholarship, and she'd spent two weeks wheedling the money out of the board, the courts, and Neville— just so William Scott could thank Charles Edward Willoughby IV for a superior education. And while she was doing all that for someone she didn't know, Corey Allen Garrett was probably getting a third-rate science education from a substitute teacher who was probably ignoring all the notes and instructions Victoria had left.

Charles, damn him, had managed to dominate her life even more dead than alive. He'd slapped his name on everything from the pencils to the rugs, on three sons and a wife, and it still wasn't enough. He'd had to go and leave his affairs in just enough of a mess that some barristers could actually make a career out of sorting through all of it, and some people—namely herself and Neville— could spend their lives fighting over it, keeping his name in the forefront of their minds and on the tips of their tongues year after year after year.

Victoria slumped to the desk, hiding her face in her arms. If she stayed in London and did what she was supposed to do, a lifetime of dry, dusty papers, old books, and fights with Neville awaited her. It had been so much easier to be ignored and shuffled off when everyone had thought Neville was the only Willoughby of consequence. Then she had an idea, an idea that had been niggling in the back of her mind for days, growing stronger and stronger with the approach of holidays she didn't want to face alone, with only J.J.'s stalwart companionship and the company of a few old, very old—nearly ancient, actually—friends she'd shared with Charles.

"Victoria." Her intercom buzzed and J.J.'s voice came over the speaker. "Don't forget. We're leaving for Spencer's in one hour to meet with Gerald Gardner and Lord Wakefield."

The room fell silent. J.J. never expected a reply unless he had a question. After a moment Victoria buzzed him back.

"I'm sorry, J.J., but I won't be able to make Spencer's this evening."

Silence fell again and lasted longer. Victoria could almost hear J.J. thinking in the other room.

"I beg your pardon, Victoria," he finally replied via the intercom, "but are you ill?"

She pushed in her button, said, "No," and let her finger slide off onto the C.E.W.IV hunter-green blotter.

"Not ill?" he asked again after a moment.

"No."

In less than a minute the door to her office opened and J.J. peeked around the jamb. "How serious is the trouble we're in? A little serious, serious, or very serious?"

"Very, very serious," she said, watching him from across a lengthy expanse of hunter-green carpet.

"Is it Fitzgerald's essay? I thought it was a bit impertinent of him to use grassland ecology, your specialty."

"No," she said. "Fitzgerald's essay is fine, but I don't think it will get him a Charles Edward Willoughby the Fourth scholarship this year, because I don't think there's going to be another one available."

J.J. only grinned. "You've underestimated yourself again, Victoria. By the time you get through with Wakefield, we'll have funded two, maybe three more of our scholarships, and gained a strong ally against Neville."

"No, J.J. The scholarships are gone, finished, and so is the Willoughby Institute."

He lifted a brow in question.

"It's over," she said.

"Over?"

"Neville is the heir. Neville can have it all," she said, stating her case as simply as possible.

J.J. hastened to disagree. "Charles never meant—"

"Charles is dead," Victoria interrupted, once again stating her case as simply as possible. Charles was dead. If he'd wanted things different than they were going to be, then he should have been more careful, more precise in his will. If he had wanted her to spend the rest of her life taking care of his name, he should have taken better care of her.

But he had not been careful, and she had been forced to find another life, a life she wanted back.

"Will you call the airline for me, J.J.?" she asked, her mind made up.

"I'd rather not," he said honestly. "I think we should talk."

"And I think I should go home." Home to the shortgrass prairie and the man she loved.

Talbot hadn't changed much in five weeks. Victoria thought she would probably think the same thing if she'd been gone five years. There was more snow than there had been at Thanksgiving, and it seemed the town and surrounding countryside would enjoy a white Christmas.

She'd picked a terrible time to return unannounced. Her house was dark and cold, and the wind was howling down out of the north, bringing a winter storm full of more snow. She didn't have a Christmas tree or any decorations hanging at the door. The school was closed, so there was no one about to chat with. She needed to call Glen Frazer first thing in the morning and let him know she was back and would return to her teaching duties on schedule. She knew he'd doubted whether she would ever return. But his doubts weren't the ones that had plagued her across the Atlantic.

Ty had let her go physically, emotionally, completely. She'd felt it in his last kiss. He was so unlike Charles, who even in death had tried to hold on to her. Of the two, she thought Ty's decision took the greater love, but her inexperience in such matters left plenty of room for confusion and doubts.

After numerous trips and untold struggling, she finally got the last of her luggage inside. She allowed herself a moment to catch her breath, then went through the house, turning on lights and turning up the heat. She'd stopped on her way out of Denver to buy groceries, knowing the store in Talbot would be closed by the time she got home. Canned soup and a grilled cheese sandwich sounded wonderful after hours on an airplane and she'd bought some pre-made cookie dough to give herself a treat.

Each time her path crossed in front of the telephone, she hesitated, wondering if it was too late to call Ty, and knowing the lateness of the hour was only an excuse to hide her fears. She'd thought about calling Lacey first and "testing the waters," to use the older woman's phrase, then decided she'd rather be a complete coward than merely half a coward.

After eating her dinner she put some cookies in the oven and set about building a fire in the fireplace. She hadn't used it before, but even with the heat on high, the house had the chill of rooms left unused for too long. When she was still cold after the fire was burning strong, she decided to take a long, hot bath. Afterward she promised herself she would call Ty, whether she'd found the courage or not.

Ty pulled his leather gloves on over a worn cotton pair and pushed his hat lower on his forehead to protect his face from the blowing snow. It was a hell of a night to be out driving around but there was little enough to do in Talbot without letting Corey miss the MacKenzies' annual Christmas party. Jake MacKenzie was Corey's best friend, and Ty knew the two boys would be up long after the other guests went home. Barbara MacKenzie had offered to bring Corey home in the morning.

She was a good woman, still pretty in her own way. He'd dated her a few times after high school. Then she'd gone and married Buck MacKenzie, and that had been the end of that.

He swung himself up into his pickup and slammed the door. The temperature was dropping toward zero. He started the truck and had to wait for it to warm up while he slowly gave the engine gas and huddled on the seat, watching the snow come down all over town. He headed for home.

On the corner of First Avenue and Third Street, Glen Frazer's house was covered in Christmas lights from stem to stern. He had a Santa Claus climbing on the roof and a choir of angels in his front yard. Every year he tried to outdo himself, and this year he'd added a sleigh and reindeer to the lawn.

The Russells had lit up their two big pine trees all the way to the top, and had a nativity scene set up on bales of hay between the two trees. Even old man Harper, way out on the edge of town, had a couple of lights strung up around his door.

The block between Second and Third streets was darker. The Martins had gone out of town for Christmas, the second house was empty, and the third—

Ty felt himself go still all over. The third house was Victoria's, and there was smoke coming out of the chimney and lights on in the windows. There had been some talk of letting the substitute science teacher have it, but the board had decided to wait until after Christmas before redoing the lease. The last Ty had heard, the substitute was using one of the trailers out behind the school.

He gave the engine a little more gas and shifted the truck into gear. He'd just drive by, he thought. Check it out. See what was going on.

He didn't really think she had come back. That was a fool's dream.

He got to the end of the block and started to drive by, then decided to stop. As long as he was there, was the theory he used to convince himself to go ahead on up to the porch. Once there, he felt bound to knock on the door and look through the living room window. If the substitute answered, a young man fresh out of college and damned grateful to have a job, Ty would make his apologies and go on home alone to face another night of trying not to think about Victoria, of trying not to be angry, because that seemed so damned futile.

No one answered his knock, and he looked through the window again. A lot of luggage was stacked in the middle of the floor, and it all had big W's on it.

She was home. He was glad and angry at the same time. He didn't know what to think until smoke began drifting out of the kitchen. Then he didn't have to think at all.

He called her name and pounded on the door before trying the knob and finding it unlocked. He rushed inside, heading for the kitchen.

Victoria heard the ruckus, and with a start realized she must have forgotten to lock the door. She'd made so many trips in and out. The sound of footsteps crossing her living room had her stumbling out of the bathtub and grabbing for a robe. As far as she knew, there had never been anyone attacked or murdered in Talbot. She would hate to go down in history as the first.

The thin cotton robe fought her wet skin, allowing her to get only one arm in a sleeve before she heard a man swear in her kitchen and call her name.

"Victoria!"

Ty! Her knees weakened, and she clutched the

robe to her breasts. Taking a deep breath, she opened the door and practically ran right into him.

"Oh."

He grabbed her arms to steady her, and the purest gray eyes she'd ever seen captured her gaze.

"Oh," she said again, softer. He was so big, towering over her with his hat shading his face, his legs braced to hold them both. She felt the cold dampness of his glove on her bare arm, while his other hand held a fistful of cotton robe and her elbow.

Ty looked down at the bared upper curves of her breasts, and his breath lodged in his throat. Straying tendrils of damp auburn hair curled around her face and clung to her ivory skin, making it near impossible for him to find his voice.

She was more beautiful than he remembered, softer than she'd been in his dreams. He'd thought about her so many times, the way she smiled, her uppity voice, the way she'd loved him in the barn the first time, and all the times after that. He'd been too long without a woman before he'd had her, and after her he'd known no other woman would do. She lit a fire in him with her shy demeanor and big brown eyes, a fire he could feel stirring again in his loins.

"Your cookies were burning," he finally said, unconsciously pulling her closer. He needed her heat against him, wanting her touch to ease the ache she'd started in his groin. "I saw the smoke coming out of the kitchen and just let myself in."

"Th-thank you."

"At first I thought it might have been the flue." His gaze drifted back down to her breasts, and this time he inhaled deeply. She felt so good, so warm and willing. He pulled her closer until she was fully against him, feeling him. "But it wasn't. Your fireplace is working fine, drawing well."

Victoria felt as scandalous as she ever had, barely out of her bath and in the arms of a fully clothed, fully aroused cowboy. She knew without a doubt what was pressing up against her belly. It was a warmer welcome than she had anticipated, and after the cold chillness of London, it was much appreciated. She smiled. She couldn't help herself.

"I missed you too." She tilted her head back to hold his gaze as color suffused her cheeks.

His tan turned darker high on his cheekbones and the barest smile curved his mouth. "Maybe we ought to do this in bed."

"Maybe we ought."

Without another word he scooped her into his arms and headed down the hall.

Making love with him was the final act of coming home. He was tender and sensual, eliciting responses she hadn't known existed inside herself until he'd first shown her. The strength and warmth of him were a haven she never wanted to leave. She'd always known home was where the heart is—she'd been given no other choice—but now she had so much more. Ty was connected to the land, to Talbot, and by loving him, she gained it all.

Afterward they baked more cookies and settled themselves in front of the roaring blaze in the fireplace. Outside, the snow was coming down thick and velvety, reflecting the moonlight and the shadows of the trees.

"How was London?" he asked, leaning forward to grab another cookie off the tray. He was terribly nonchalant, but she heard the underlying questions, and possibly the doubts.

"Cold and snowy," she said, burrowing deeper into the blankets they'd brought out from the bed.

"Kind of like Talbot, then." He looked over his shoulder at her and grinned.

"No." She wrinkled her nose. "London is a little bigger, and there're a couple more people crowding the streets. Some of the buildings are taller, and there's a palace or two. Nothing special."

"Guess it will all keep until you get back, huh?" His tone was light, but his eyes were solemn and serious beneath the dark slashes of his eyebrows.

"It better do better than that. I'm not planning on going back."

He nodded. "You must have saved Charles's place in history."

"No. I didn't. He's going to have to count on Neville to do that for him. I'm not going to be a Willoughby much longer."

That got his attention. He turned to face her fully. "What's your plan?"

"Well, my maiden name was Cameron, and I've decided to use it. Victoria Miranda Elizabeth Cameron. What do you think?"

"It's got a nice ring to it, I suppose," he said, not sounding overly enthused.

They sat quietly on the couch for a few minutes, each lost in thought, until Victoria couldn't hold back any longer.

"I'm open to suggestions," she said softly.

He took a deep breath and turned to look her straight in the eye. "Garrett," he said. "Your name ought to be Garrett. Victoria Miranda Elizabeth Garrett."

As a marriage proposal, it was about the worst he'd ever heard. It was certainly worse than he'd imagined it a hundred times. He'd had so many good ways of asking her. He winced at the awfulness of it and swore quietly under his breath.

"Garrett?" she repeated. "Victoria Garrett. Wouldn't that confuse everybody? What with us both having the same name?"

"Not if we were married," he said bluntly, not liking his second shot at a proposal any more than his first.

"Oh, I see." She smiled a secret smile, teasing him. "Yes, I think that would be best. Keep everything above board and all that."

"Then it's settled?"

"Quite settled." Her smile lingered, softening the formality of her words.

"It's me, and the ranch, and Corey, the whole package deal," he said, determined to give her a way out even as he wanted to hold her to him and never let her go.

"A bargain, I'm sure."

"And more kids, at least a couple." He hoped she felt the same way. He'd love to have children with her.

"You will have my utmost cooperation in the progeny department."

Sounded good to him. A wide grin spread across his face. "You're going to marry me, Victoria."

"Yes," she said, her eyes bright with promise. "I'm going to marry you, Ty Garrett."

His grin broadened. "There's something else you ought to know." He sat back, pulling her into his arms and kissing her. "I've been in love with you since that first night I picked you up and got that button tangled in your hair. I wanted to make love to you right then and there."

"I would have fainted dead away, I'm sure." She kissed him back, letting her tongue taste his lips.

He responded by plundering her mouth and filling his palm with her breast. When he lifted his head, he said, "I haven't noticed you getting faint on me lately."

"Since then I've learned how to handle an American cowboy." She scooted closer, nestling herself against him.

"And how's that?" he asked, taking full advantage of her new position. He kissed her again, slow and sweet.

"Well," she answered breathlessly, warming to his touch and the reality that he was hers for a lifetime. "First you fall in love. The rest comes easy after that."

Ty chuckled and buried his face in the soft, tantalizing curve of her neck. His tongue darted out to taste the fresh sweetness of her skin. "It's going to be a long, snow-packed winter this year, honey."

"Good," she murmured, imagining warm nights in front of their fireplace and hot nights in bed, crisp days spent helping him and Corey doing chores, and cold mornings when they all shared coffee and cocoa to get warm.

"It's going to be a good life, Victoria." His voice was warm and solid, his promise as strong as the man.

"Yes, it is, Ty. Yes, it is."

THE EDITOR'S CORNER

It's summertime, and nothing makes the living as easy—and exciting—as knowing that next month six terrific LOVESWEPTs are coming your way. Whether you decide to take them to the beach or your backyard hammock, these novels, written by your favorite authors, are guaranteed to give you hours of sheer pleasure.

Lynne Bryant leads the line-up with **BELIEVING HEART**, LOVESWEPT #630—and one tall, dark, and dangerously handsome hero. Duke King is head of his family's oil company, a man nobody dares to cross, so the last thing he expects is to be shanghaied by a woman! Though Marnie MacBride knows it's reckless to rescue this mogul from a kidnapping attempt single-handedly, she has no choice but to save him. When she sails off with him in her boat, she fancies herself his protector; little does she know that under the magic of a moonlit sky, serious, responsible Duke will throw caution to the wind and, like a swashbuckling pirate, lay claim to the potent pleasures of her lips. Marnie makes Duke think of a seductive sea witch, a feisty Venus, and he's captivated by the sweet magic of her spirit. He wishes he could give her a happy ending to their adventure together, but he knows he can never be what she wants most. And Marnie finds she has to risk all to heal his secret pain, to teach his heart to believe in dreams once more. Lynne has written a beautiful, shimmering love story.

With **ALL FOR QUINN**, LOVESWEPT #631, Kay Hooper ends her *Men of Mysteries Past* series on an unforgettable note—and a truly memorable hero. You've seen Quinn in action in the previous three books of the series, and if you're like any red-blooded woman, you've already lost your heart to this green-eyed prince of thieves. Morgan West certainly has, and that lands her in a bit of a pickle, since Quinn's expected to rob the Mysteries Past exhibit of priceless jewelry at the museum she runs. But how could she help falling under his sensual spell? Quinn's an international outlaw with charm, wit, and intelligence who, in the nine and a half weeks since they have met, has stolen a necklace right off her neck, given her the mocking gift of a concubine ring, then turned up on her doorstep wounded and vulnerable, trusting her with his life. Even as she's being enticed beyond reason, Quinn is chancing a perilous plan that can cost him her love. Pick up a copy and treat yourself to Kay at her absolute best!

Ruth Owen made quite a splash when Einstein, the jive-talking, TV-shopping computer from her first LOVESWEPT, **MELTDOWN**, won a special WISH (Women in Search of a Hero) award from *Romantic Times*. Well, in **SMOOTH OPERATOR**, LOVESWEPT #632, Einstein is back, and this time he has a sister computer with a problem. PINK loves to gamble, you see, and this keeps Katrina Sheffield on her toes. She's in charge of these two super-intelligent machines, and as much as the independent beauty hates to admit it, she needs help containing PINK's vice. Only one person is good enough to involve in this situation—Jack Fagen, the security whiz they call the Terminator. He's a ruthless troubleshooter, the kind of man every mother warns her daughter about, and though Kat should know better, she can't deny that his heat brands her with wildfire. When it becomes obvious that someone is trying to destroy all she's worked for, she has no choice but to rely on Jack to prove her innocence. Superbly combining humor and sensuality, Ruth delivers a must-read.

STORMY WEATHER, LOVESWEPT #633, by Gail Douglas, is an apt description for the turbulent state Mitch Canfield finds himself in from the moment Tiffany Greer enters his life. Though she isn't wearing a sarong and lei when he first catches sight of her, he knows instantly who the pretty woman is. The native Hawaiian has come to Winnipeg in the winter to check out his family's farm for her company, but she's got all the wrong clothes and no idea how cold it can be. Though he doubts she'll last long in the chilly north, he can't help feeling possessive or imagining what it would be like to cuddle with her beside a raging fire—and ignite a few of his own. It seems he's spending half his time making serious promises to himself to keep his hands off her, and the other half breaking those promises. Tiffany wants to keep her mind on business, but she's soon distracted by the cool beauty of the land around her and exhilarated by Mitch's potent kisses. Then she runs into the impenetrable barrier of his mysterious hurt, and she knows she's facing the biggest challenge of her life—to convince Mitch that his arms are the only place she'll ever feel warm again. Gail's luminous writing is simply irresistible.

If intensity is what you've come to expect from a novel by Laura Taylor, then **HEARTBREAKER**, LOVESWEPT #634, will undoubtedly satisfy you. After an explosion renders Naval Intelligence officer Micah Holbrook sightless, he turns furious, hostile, desperate to seize control of his life—and also more magnificently handsome than ever, Bliss Rowland decides. Ever since he saved her life years ago, she's compared every other man she's ever met to him, and no one has measured up. Now that he's come to the island of St. Thomas to begin his recuperation under her care, the last thing she intends to allow is for him to surrender to his fear. It's hard fighting for a man who doesn't want to fight to get better, and the storm of emotions that engulfs them both threatens to destroy her soul. Unsure of his recovery, Micah keeps pushing her away, determined to ignore his hunger to caress her silken skin and the taste of longing on her lips. Knowing that only her passion can heal his pain, Bliss dares him to be conquered by his need. Laura will touch your heart with this stunning love story.

Last, but certainly not least, in the line-up is **CON MAN** by Maris Soule, LOVESWEPT #635. As head of a foundation that provides money for worthy causes, Kurt Jones is definitely no con man, but he knows that's how Micki Bradford will think of him once she learns of his deception. It all starts when, instead of letting his usual investigator check out a prospective grant recipient, he decides he'll try undercover work himself. He arranges a meeting with expert rider Micki, then on the pretense that he's interested in finding a stable for a horse, pumps her for information . . . even as his gaze caresses her and he longs to touch her as she's never been touched. He's tempted to tell her the truth, to promise he'll never hurt her, but Micki has learned the hard way how irresistible a good-looking liar can be. As Kurt sweeps her into a steamy charade to unearth the facts, Kurt vows he'd dare any danger to win Micki's trust, and teach her to have faith in his love. Maris does nothing less than thrill you with this exciting romance.

On sale this month from Bantam are two thrilling novels of passion and intrigue. First is **LADY VALIANT** by the magnificent Suzanne Robinson, whom *Romantic Times* has described as "an author with star quality." In this mesmerizing tale of grand romantic adventure, Thea Hunt is determined to repay the kindness of Mary, Queen of Scots, by journeying to Scotland to warn her away from a treacherous marriage. But in the thick of an English forest, she suddenly finds herself set upon by thieves . . . and chased down by a golden-haired highwayman who stills her struggles—and stirs her heart—with one penetrating glance from his fiery blue eyes. As a spy in Queen Elizabeth's service, Robin St. John is prepared to despise Thea, whom he considers a traitorous wench, to enjoy her torment as he spirits her away to a castle where she'll remain until Mary Stuart is safely wed. But he finds himself desiring her more than any other woman he's ever met. As captive and captor clash, Robin vows to use his every weapon to make Thea surrender to the raging fires of his need and the rising heat of her own passion.

Lois Wolfe returns with **MASK OF NIGHT**, a tantalizing historical romance where one bewitching actress finds love and danger waiting in the wings. Katie Henslowe's prayers are answered the night wealthy railroad tycoon Julian Gates becomes her benefactor, hiring her family's ragtag acting troupe for his new theater. But no sooner has her uncertain world begun to settle down than the potent kiss of a maddeningly attractive stranger sends her reeling. Matt Dennigan is arrogant, enigmatic, and broke—reasons enough for Katie to avoid him. And when, for secret motives of his own, the mysterious rancher begins to draw her into his search for evidence again Julian, Katie tries to resist. But in Matt's heated embrace she finds herself giving in to her innermost longings, only to discover that she and Matt are trapped in a treacherous quest for justice. Against all odds they become partners in a dangerous mission that will take them from a teeming city to the wild frontier, testing the limits of their courage and turning their fiercest desires into spellbinding love. . . .

Also on sale this month, in the hardcover edition from Doubleday, is **SATIN AND STEELE** by the ever-popular Fayrene Preston. Long out of print, this is a wonderfully evocative and uniquely contemporary love story. Skye Anderson knows the joy and wonder of love, as well as the pain of its tragic loss. She's carved a new life for herself at Dallas's Hayes Corporation, finding security in a cocoon of hardworking days and lonely nights. Then her company is taken over by the legendary corporate raider James Steele, and once again Skye must face the possibility of losing everything she cares about. When Steele enlists her aid in organizing the new corporation, she's determined to prove herself worthy of the challenge. But as they work together side by side, she can't deny that she feels more than a professional interest in her new boss—and that the feeling is mutual. Soon she'll have to decide whether to let go of her desire for Steele once and for all—or to risk everything for a second chance at love.

Happy reading!

With warmest wishes,

Nita Taublib

Associate Publisher

Don't miss these exciting books by your
favorite Bantam authors

On sale in June:
LADY VALIANT
by Suzanne Robinson

MASK OF NIGHT
by Lois Wolfe

And in hardcover from Doubleday
SATIN AND STEELE
by Fayrene Preston

From the bestselling author of
Lady Defiant, Lady Hellfire, and
Lady Gallant . . .

Suzanne Robinson

"An author with star
quality . . . spectacularly talented."
—*Romantic Times*

Lady Valiant

Breathtakingly talented author Suzanne Robinson spins a richly romantic new historical romance set during the spellbinding Elizabethan era. LADY VALIANT is the passionate love story of Rob Savage—highwayman, nobleman, and master spy—and the fiery young beauty he kidnaps.

A tantalizing glimpse follows . . .

Thea Hunt refused to ride in the coach. Heavy, cumbersome, and slow, it jounced her so that she nearly vomited after a few minutes inside it. She preferred riding at the head of her party, just behind the outriders, in spite of Nan Hobby's objections. Hobby rode in the coach and shouted at her charge whenever she felt Thea was riding too fast.

"Miiiiiistress!"

Thea groaned and turned her mare. There was no use trying to ignore Hobby. It only made her shout louder. As the outriders entered the next valley, Thea pulled alongside the coach. The vehicle jolted over a log, causing Hobby to disappear in a flurry of skirts and petticoats.

"Aaaoow," groaned Hobby. "Mistress, my bones, my bones."

"You could ride."

"That horrible mare you gave me can't be trusted."

"Not when you shriek at her and scare her into bolting."

"Aaaaow."

Thea pointed down the track that led into the oak-and-hazel-wooded valley. "We'll be following this road. No more spiny hills for a while."

She glanced up at the hills on either side of the valley. Steeply pitched like tent tops they posed a hazard to the wagons, loaded with chests and furniture, and to the coach. Yet she was glad to see them, for their presence meant northern England. Soon they would reach the border and Scotland. She heard the call of a lapwing in the distance and spotted a merlin overhead. The countryside seemed deserted except for their small party.

She'd insisted on taking as few servants and men-at-arms as necessary in order to travel quickly. She and Hobby were the only women and the men-at-arms numbered only seven including her steward. Still, the baggage and Hobby slowed them down, and she had need of haste.

The Queen of Scots was to marry that fool Darnley. When Grandmother told her the news, at first she hadn't believed it. Clever, beautiful, and softhearted, Her Majesty deserved better than that selfish toad. Thea had pondered long upon Grandmother's suggestion that she go to Scotland. Grandmother said Mary Stuart would listen to no criticism of Darnley, but that she might listen to Thea. After all, they had both shared quarters and tutors with the French royal children.

Thea had been honored with Mary's friendship, for both found themselves foreigners among a clutch of French children. Later, when Thea had need of much more than friendship, Mary had given her aid, had seen to it that Thea was allowed to go home.

Slapping her riding crop on her leg, Thea muttered to herself. "Don't think of it. That time is over. You'll go to Scotland for a time and then return to the country where no one can hurt you."

Nudging her mare, she resumed her place near the front of the line of horses and wagons. Only a cause of great moment could have forced her to leave her seclusion. She'd made her own life far away from any young noblemen. Some called her a hermit. Some accused her of false pride. None suspected the mortal wound she nursed in secret—a wound so grievous and humiliating it had sent her flying from the French court determined to quit the society of the highborn forever.

Her steward interrupted her thoughts. "Mistress, it's close to midday. Shall I look for a place to stop?"

She nodded and the man trotted ahead. Hunger had crept up on her unnoticed, and she tugged at the collar of her riding gown. Her finger caught the edge of one of the gold buttons that ran down the garment, and she felt a sting. Grimacing, she looked at her forefinger. Blood beaded up in a small cut on the side. She sucked the wound and vowed to demand that Hobby remove the buttons. They'd been a gift from Grandmother, but one of them had a sharp edge that needed filing.

It was a good excuse to replace them with the old, plainer buttons she preferred. These were too ornate for her taste. She always felt she should be wearing brocade or velvet with them, and a riding hat, which she detested. Only this morning Hobby had tried to convince her to wear one of those silly jeweled and feathered contrivances on her head. Refusing, she'd stuffed her thick black hair into a net that kept the straight locks out of her way.

She examined her finger. It had stopped bleeding. Pulling her gloves from her belt, she drew them on and searched the path ahead for signs of the steward's return. As she looked past the first outrider, something dropped on the man from the overhanging branches like an enormous fruit with appendages. The second outrider dropped under the weight of another missile and at the same time she heard shouts and grunts from the man behind her.

"Aaaaow! Murder, murder!"

A giant attacked the coach, lumbering over to it and thrusting his arms inside. A scrawny man in a patched cloak toppled into her path as she turned her horse toward the coach. He sprang erect and pointed at her.

"Here, Robin!"

She looked in the direction of the man's gaze and saw a black stallion wheel, his great bulk easily controlled by a golden-haired man who seemed a part of the animal. The stallion and his rider jumped into motion, hooves tearing the earth, the man's long body aligning itself over the horse's neck. Stilled by fright, she watched him control the animal with a strength that seemed to rival that of the stallion.

The brief stillness vanished as she understood that the man who was more stallion than human was coming for her. Fear lanced through her. She kicked her mare hard and sprang away, racing down the path through the trees. Riding sidesaddle, she had a precarious perch, but she tapped her mare with the crop, knowing that the risk of capture by a highwayman outweighed the risk of a fall. Her heart pounding with the hoofbeats of her mare, she fled.

The path twisted to the right and she nearly lost her seat as she rounded the turn. Righting herself, she felt the mare stretch her legs out and saw that the way had straightened. She leaned over her horse, not daring to look behind and lose her balance. Thus she only heard the thunder of hooves and felt the spray of dirt as the stallion caught up. The animal's black head appeared, and she kicked her mare in desperation.

A gloved hand appeared, then a golden head. An arm snaked out and encircled her waist. Thea sailed out of the saddle and landed in front of the highwayman. Terror gave her strength. She wriggled and pounded the imprisoning arm.

"None of that, beastly papist gentry mort."

Understanding little of this, caring not at all, Thea wriggled harder and managed to twist so that she could bite the highwayman's arm. She was rewarded with a howl. Twisting again, she bit the hand that snatched at her hair and thrust herself out of the saddle as the stallion was slowing to a trot.

She landed on her side, rolled, and scrambled to her feet. Ahead she could see her mare walking down the trail in search of grass. Sprinting for the animal, she felt her hair come loose from its net and sail out behind her. Only a few yards and she might escape on the mare.

Too late she heard the stallion. She glanced over her shoulder to see a scowling face. She gave a little yelp as a long, lean body sailed at her. She turned to leap out of range, but the highwayman landed on her. The force of his weight jolted the air from her lungs and she fell. The ground jumped at her face. Her head banged against something. There was a moment of sharp pain and the feeling of smothering before she lost her senses altogether.

Her next thought wasn't quite a thought, for in truth there was room in her mind for little more than feeling. Her head ached. She was queasy and she couldn't summon the strength to open her eyes. She could feel her face because someone had laid a palm against her cheek. She could feel her hand, because someone was holding it.

"Wake you, my prize. I've no winding sheet to wrap you in if you die."

The words were harsh. It was the voice of thievery and rampage, the voice of a masterless man, a highwayman. Her eyes flew open at the thought and met the sun. No, not the sun, bright light filtered through a mane of long, roughly cut tresses. She shifted her gaze to the man's face and saw his lips curve into a smile of combined satisfaction and derision. She could only lie on the ground and blink at him, waiting.

He leaned toward her and she shrank away. Glaring at her, he held her so that she couldn't retreat. He came close, and she was about to scream when he touched the neck of her gown. The feel of his gloved hand on her throat took her voice from her. She began to shake. An evil smile appeared upon his lips, then she felt a tightening of her collar and a rip. She found her voice and screamed as he tore the top button from her gown. Flailing at him weakly, she drew breath to scream again, but he clamped a hand over her mouth.

"Do you want me to stuff my gloves into your mouth?"

She stared at him, trapped by his grip and the malice in his dark blue eyes.

"Do you?"

She shook her head.

"Then keep quiet."

He removed his hand and she squeezed her eyes shut, expecting him to resume his attack. When nothing happened, she peeped at him from beneath her lashes. He was regarding her with a contemptuous look, but soon transferred his gaze to the button in his palm. He pressed it between his fingers, frowned at it, then shoved it into a pouch at his belt.

"I'll have the rest of them later," he said.

Reaching for her, he stopped when she shrank from him. He hesitated, then grinned at her.

"Sit you up by yourself then."

Still waiting for him to pounce on her, she moved her arms, but when she tried to shove herself erect, she found them useless. He snorted. Gathering her in his arms, he raised her to a sitting position. She winced at the pain in her head. His hand came up to cradle her cheek and she moaned.

"If you puke on me I'll tie you face down on your horse for the ride home."

Fear gave way to anger. In spite of her pain, she shoved at his chest. To her chagrin, what she thought were mortal blows turned out to be taps.

"Aaaow! Look what you've done to my lady."

"Get you gone, you old cow. She's well and will remain so, for now. Stubb, put the maid on a horse and let's fly. No sense waiting here for company any longer."

Thea opened her eyes. The highwayman was issuing orders to his ruffians. From her position she could see the day's growth of beard on his chin and the tense cords of muscle in his neck.

"My—my men."

"Will have a long walk," he snapped.

"Leave us," she whispered, trying to sit up. "You have your booty."

The highwayman moved abruptly to kneel in front of her. Taking her by the shoulders, he pulled her so that they faced each other eye to eye.

"But Mistress Hunt, you are the booty. All the rest is fortune's addition."

"But—"

He ignored her. Standing quickly, he picked her up. Made dizzy by the sudden change, she allowed her head to drop to his shoulder. She could smell the leather of his jerkin and feel the soft cambric of his shirt. An outlaw who wore cambric shirts.

She was transferred to the arms of another ruffian, a wiry man no taller than she with a crooked nose and a belligerent expression. Her captor mounted the black stallion again and reached down.

"Give her to me."

Lifted in front of the highwayman, she was settled in his lap a great distance from the ground. The stallion danced sideways and his master put a steadying hand on the animal's neck. The stallion calmed at once.

"Now, Mistress Hunt, shall I tie your hands, or will you behave? I got no patience for foolish gentry morts who don't know better than to try outrunning horses."

Anger got the better of her. "You may be sure the next time I leave I'll take your horse."

"God's blood, woman. You take him, and I'll give you the whipping you've asked for."

His hand touched a whip tied to his saddle and she believed him. She screamed and began to struggle.

"Cease your nattering, woman."

He fastened his hand over her mouth again. His free arm wrapped around her waist. Squeezing her against his hard body, he stifled her cries. When she went limp from lack of air, he released her.

"Any more yowling and I'll gag you."

Grabbing her by the shoulders, he drew her close so that she was forced to look into his eyes. Transfixed by their scornful beauty, she remained silent.

"What say you?" he asked. "Shall I finish what I began and take all your buttons?"

Hardly able to draw breath, she hadn't the strength to move her lips.

"Answer, woman. Will you ride quietly, or fight beneath me on the ground again?"

"R—ride."

Chuckling he turned her around so that her back was to his chest and called to his men. The outlaw called Stubb rode up leading a horse carrying Hobby, and Thea twisted her head around to see if her maid fared well.

"Look here, Rob Savage," Stubb said. "If you want to scrap with the gentry mort all day, I'm going on. No telling when someone else is going to come along, and I'm not keen on another fight this day."

"Give me a strap then."

A strap. He was going to beat her. Thea gasped and rammed her elbow into Rob's stomach. She writhed and twisted, trying to escape the first blow from the lash. Rob finally trapped her by fastening his arms about her and holding her arms to her body.

"Quick, Stubb, tie her hands with the strap."

Subsiding, Thea bit her lower lip. Her struggles had been for naught. Rob's arm left her, but he shook her by the shoulders.

"Now be quiet or I'll tie you to a pack horse."

"Aaaow! Savage, Robin Savage, the highwayman. God preserve us. We're lost, lost. Oh, mistress, it's Robin Savage. He's killed hundreds of innocent souls. He kills babes and ravages their mothers and steals food from children and burns churches and dismembers clergymen and—"

Thea felt her body grow cold and heavy at the same time. She turned and glanced up at the man who held her. He was frowning at the hysterical Hobby. Suddenly he looked down at her. One of his brows lifted and he smiled slowly.

"A body's got to have a calling."

"You—you've done these things?"

"Now how's a man to remember every little trespass and sin, especially a man as busy as me?"

He grinned at her, lifted a hand to his men, and kicked the stallion. Her head was thrown back against his chest. He steadied her with an arm around her waist, but she squirmed away from him. He ignored her efforts and pulled her close as the horse sprang into a gallop. She grasped his arm with her bound hands, trying to pry it loose to no avail. It was as much use for a snail to attempt to move a boulder.

The stallion leaped over a fallen sapling and she clutched at Savage's arm. Riding a small mare was a far less alarming experience than trying to keep her seat on this black giant. She would have to wait for a chance to escape, but escape she must.

This man was a villain with a price on his head. She remembered hearing of him now. He and his band roamed the highways of England doing murder and thievery at will. Savage would appear, relieve an honest nobleman or merchant of his wealth and vanish. No sheriff or constable could find him.

As they rode, Thea mastered her fears enough to begin to think. This man wanted more than just riches and rape. If he'd only wanted these things, he could have finished his attack when he'd begun it. And it wasn't as if she were tempting to men, a beauty worth keeping. She'd found that out long ago in France. And this Savage knew her name. The mystery calmed her somewhat. Again she twisted, daring a glance at him.

"Why have you abducted me?"

He gaped at her for a moment before returning his gaze to the road ahead. "For the same reason I take any woman. For using."

He slowed the stallion and turned off the road. Plunging into the forest, they left behind the men assigned to bring the coach and wagons. Several thieves went ahead, while Stubb and the rest followed their master. Thea summoned her courage to break the silence once more.

"Why else?"

"What?"

"It can't be the only reason, to, to . . ."

"Why not?"

"You know my name. You were looking for me, not for just anyone."

"Is that so?"

"Are you going to hold me for ransom? There are far richer prizes than me."

"Ransom. Now there's a right marvelous idea. Holding a woman for ransom's a pleasureful occupation."

As he leered down at her, fear returned. Her body shook. She swallowed and spoke faintly.

"No."

There was a sharp gasp of exasperation from Savage. "Don't you be telling me what I want."

"But you can't."

His gaze ran over her face and hair. The sight appeared to anger him, for he cursed and snarled at her.

"Don't you be telling me what I can do. God's blood, woman, I could throw you down and mount you right here."

She caught her lower lip between her teeth, frozen into her own horror by his threats. He snarled at her again and turned her away from him, holding her shoulders so that she couldn't face him. Though he used only the strength of his hands, it was enough to control her, which frightened her even more.

"I could do it," he said. "I might if you don't keep quiet. Mayhap being mounted a few times would shut you up."

Thea remained silent, not daring to anger him further. She had no experience of villains. This one had hurt her. He might hurt her worse. She must take him at his word, despite her suspicion that he'd planned to hold her for ransom. She must escape. She must escape with Hobby and find her men.

They rode for several hours through fells and dales, always heading south, deeper into England. She pondered hard upon how to escape as they traveled. Freeing herself from Savage was impossible. He was too strong and wary of her after her first attempt. She might request a stop to relieve herself, but the foul man might insist upon watching her. No, she would have to wait until they stopped for the night and hope he didn't tie her down.

Her gorge rose at the thought of what he might do once they stopped. She tried to stop her body from trembling, but failed. Her own helplessness frightened her and she struggled not to let tears fall. If she didn't escape, she would fight. It seemed to be her way, to keep fighting no matter how useless the struggle.

As dusk fell they crossed a meadow and climbed a rounded hill. At the top she had a view of the countryside. Before her stretched a great forest, its trees so thick she could see nothing but an ocean of leaves.

Savage led his men down the hillside and into the forest. As they entered, the sun faded into a twilight caused by the canopy of leaves about them. Savage rode on until the twilight had almost vanished. Halting in a clearing by a noisy stream, he lifted Thea down.

She'd been on the horse so long and the hours of fear had wearied her so much that her legs buckled under her. Savage caught her, his hands coming up under her arms, and she stumbled against him. Clutching her, he swore. She looked up at him to find him glaring at her again. She caught her breath, certain he would leap upon her.

His arms tightened about her, but he didn't throw her to the ground. Instead, he stared at her. Too confused at the moment to be afraid, she stared back. Long moments passed while they gazed at each other, studying, wary, untrusting.

When he too seemed caught in a web of reverie her fears gradually eased. Eyes of gentian blue met hers and she felt a stab of pain. To her surprise, looking at him had caused the pain. Until that moment she hadn't realized a man's mere appearance could delight to the point of pain.

It was her first long look at him free of terror. Not in all her years in the fabulous court of France had she seen such a man. Even his shoulders were muscled. They were wide in contrast to his hips and he was taller than any Frenchman. He topped any of his thievish minions and yet seemed unaware of the effect of his appearance. Despite his angelic coloring, however, he had the disposition of an adder. He was scowling at her, as if something had caught him unprepared and thus annoyed him. Wariness and fear rushed to the fore again.

"Golden eyes and jet black hair. Why did you have to be so—God's blood, woman." He thrust her away from him. "Never you mind. You were right anyway, little papist. I'm after ransom."

Bewildered, she remained where she was while he stalked away from her. He turned swiftly to point at her.

"Don't you think of running. If I have to chase you and

wrestle with you again, you'll pay in any way I find amusing."
He marched off to shout ill-tempered orders at his men.

Hobby trotted up to her and began untying the leather strap
that bound her hands. Thea stared at Robin Savage, frightened
once more and eyeing his leather-clad figure. How could she have
forgotten his cruelty and appetite simply because he had a lush,
well-formed body and eyes that could kindle wet leaves? She
watched him disappear into the trees at the edge of the clearing,
and at last she was released from the bondage of his presence.

"He's mad," she said.

"Mad, of course, he's mad," Hobby said. "He's a thief and
a murderer and a ravager."

"How could God create such a man, so—so pleasing to the
eye and so evil of spirit?"

"Take no fantasy about this one, mistress. He's a foul villain
who'd as soon slit your throat as spit on you."

"I know." Thea bent and whispered to Hobby. "Can you
run fast and long? We must fly this night. Who knows what will
happen to us once he's done settling his men."

"I can run."

"Good. I'll watch for my chance and you do as well." She
looked around at the men caring for horses and making a fire.
Stubb watched them as he unloaded saddlebags. "For now, I
must find privacy."

Hobby pointed to a place at the edge of the clearing where
bushes grew thick. They walked toward it unhindered. Hobby
stopped at the edge of the clearing to guard Thea's retreat. Thea
plunged into the trees looking for the thickest bushes. Thrusting a low-hanging branch aside, she rounded an oak tree. A tall
form blocked her way. Before she could react, she was thrust
against the tree, and a man's body pressed against hers.

Robin Savage held her fast, swearing at her. She cast a
frightened glance at him, but he wasn't looking at her. He was
absorbed in studying her lips. His anger had faded and his
expression took on a somnolent turbulence. He leaned close and
whispered in her ear, sending chills down her spine.

"Running away in spite of my warnings, little papist."

Thea felt a leg shove between her thighs. His chest pressed
against her breasts, causing her to pant. He stared into her eyes
and murmured.

"Naughty wench. Now I'll have to punish you."

Mask of Night
by
Lois Wolfe

author of *The Schemers*

A spectacular new historical romance that combines breath-taking intrigue and suspense with breathless passion.

She was an actress who made her living spinning dreams. He was a rancher turned spy whose dreams had all been bitterly broken. Against all odds, they became partners in a dangerous mission that would take them from the teeming city to the wild frontier, testing the limits of their courage, and turning their fiercest desires into spellbinding love . . .

Read on for a taste of this unforgettable tale.

What use Gates might have for Katie was immediately apparent when Matt saw her emerge from the cloakroom in an under-stated emerald green gown. He made note of the dress, especially the top of it, the part that wasn't there. Nice swoop.

Real nice swoop.

Other men noticed too, as she crossed the lobby to the front desk. Matt debated following her. He was already late for dinner with the Senator, but, hell, a little more close observation couldn't hurt.

He joined her at the front desk. Her expression showed annoyance the moment she saw him, and he guessed she regretted trying to be polite to him.

"Looks like we both have business here," he said, leaning on the counter.

She turned her back on him, leaving him free to study her, the indignant thrust of her shoulders, the fragile trough of her spine. A wisp of dark golden hair had escaped its pin and rested in the curve of her neck.

"I'm here to meet my brother, Edmund Henslowe," she told the desk clerk.

The clerk went off to check the message boxes. She cocked her chin to her shoulder and sent Matt a withering look.

Hazel, he thought. Her eyes were hazel, more green than brown.

"Miss Katie Henslowe?" the clerk asked when he returned. "Mr. Henslowe wishes you to join him in his suite."

She was obviously startled. "His suite? Here?"

"Sixth floor. Number nineteen."

Six nineteen, Matt thought, looking ahead and not at her.

"Thank you." Icy, perfunctory. She was miffed.

The clerk had business at the other end of the long front desk, and they were alone for a moment.

She stood silent awhile, then turned to Matt. "Did you get all that?"

He was cautious. "What?"

"Don't play dumb. It looks too natural on you. Nice piece of news, wasn't it? The fact that my brother has a room here? Makes it seem like he has money, doesn't it? Well, let me assure you, you and whichever of our creditors you're the snoop for, Poppy does *not* have funds to make payments."

Matt played along, glancing around the opulent lobby. "This doesn't exactly look like a place for the destitute."

"I know." She backed down, stiffly. "Just, please, try to understand. My brother is here only to develop resources for the troupe. Now, I'm sure your loan department will be glad to hear that we may have the potential to resume quarterly payments." She paused. "You *are* a bank agent for Philadelphia Savings, aren't you?"

He shook his head.

"New York Fiduciary?"

"No."

"You work in the private sector, then, for an individual?"

"You could say that."

She looked away. "It's about Edmund, isn't it?"

"How'd you guess?"

Her glance took in his unfashionable attire and worn shoes. "My brother tends to attract an eclectic and, sometimes, illicit crowd."

"Which one am I? Eclectic or illicit?"

"You're a coward and a spy, and I doubt that you've got enough grapeshot in the bag to so much as fire off your name."

He looked at her for a long time. "Insults like that don't come from a lady."

"No." She held his gaze. "And they don't apply to a gentleman."

"Look, I'm not one of your brother's Jack Nasty lowlifes."

"You're not? And yet you have business here?" She studied him thoughtfully. "Are you meeting the senator then?"

Christ, how'd she know? He felt himself grow stony-faced, trying to keep reaction to a minimum.

"I remember," she went on, "seeing you waylay the distinguished senator backstage, Mr. . . . ?" She waited again for his name.

"Nasty," he said curtly. "Jack Nasty."

"I thought so."

To his surprise, she sidled close and put a hand on his arm. "Sir?" she called to the desk clerk. "My friend here has a request."

Matt tensed. What was she doing?

"Yes, sir?" the clerk asked, returning to them.

"He needs his messages," Katie interjected before Matt could speak.

"Of course." The clerk turned to Matt. "What is the name?"

Damn her.

She smiled prettily at him. "Now, come on. Don't dawdle," she said, as to a child. "You'll make us both late."

He hated being manipulated. He especially hated a woman who did it so well.

She patted his hand. "I know you've had a terrible sore throat." She turned to the clerk. "Maybe if you could just lean close, so he can whisper."

The clerk looked dubious, but obligingly leaned over the counter.

Matt felt pressure rise inside him like steam in a boiler.

"Still hurts?" she asked. "Would it be easier if you just spel it? I'm sure–"

"Dennigan!" The word shot out from between gritte teeth.

The clerk stared, astonished.

Katie removed her hand from his. "See how much bette you sound when you try?" she said, then turned to the clerk "Please check the message box for Mr. Dennigan."

Matt leaned close so no one would see him grab her wrist grab it hard. "Dennigan," he repeated. "Matt Dennigan."

"Charmed, I'm sure."

She jerked her arm free as the clerk returned. His manne was noticeably more unctuous toward Matt. "Mr. Dennigan? I seems Senator Cahill is waiting dinner for you in the Walke Room."

"The Walker Room," Katie said. "Isn't that the salon fo very private dining?"

The clerk nodded again. "Yes, ma'am. Right through th arch and turn left."

Katie looked at Matt. "Well, now, Matt, enjoy your din ner."

She was gracious in triumph, almost sweet, he thought a she left him. She hurried to the elevator foyer. He stood a long while, watching until the accordion gate of the elevator col lapsed sideways to let her on.

She had taken his amateurish game of sleuth and, in on polished play, raised the ante to life-or-death for the Senator' investigation. If she dared mention Matt Dennigan and Senator Cahill in the same breath to the cutthroat million aire she was about to meet, the game was over. Julian Gate would run for cover and retaliate with all the congressiona influence—and hired guns—his money could buy.

Jesus Christ.

CALL JAN SPILLER'S ASTROLINE

OFFICIAL RULES

To enter the sweepstakes below carefully follow all instructions found elsewhere in this offer.

The **Winners Classic** will award prizes with the following approximate maximum values: 1 Grand Prize: $26,500 (or $25,000 cash alternate); 1 First Prize: $3,000; 5 Second Prizes: $400 each; 35 Third Prizes: $100 each; 1,000 Fourth Prizes: $7.50 each. Total maximum retail value of Winners Classic Sweepstakes is $42,500. Some presentations of this sweepstakes may contain individual entry numbers corresponding to one or more of the aforementioned prize levels. To determine the Winners, individual entry numbers will first be compared with the winning numbers preselected by computer. For winning numbers not returned, prizes will be awarded in random drawings from among all eligible entries received. Prize choices may be offered at various levels. If a winner chooses an automobile prize, all license and registration fees, taxes, destination charges and, other expenses not offered herein are the responsibility of the winner. If a winner chooses a trip, travel must be complete within one year from the time the prize is awarded. Minors must be accompanied by an adult Travel companion(s) must also sign release of liability. Trips are subject to space and departure availability. Certain black-out dates may apply.

The following applies to the sweepstakes named above:

No purchase necessary. You can also enter the sweepstakes by sending your name and address to: P.O. Box 508, Gibbstown, N.J. 08027. Mail each entry separately. Sweepstakes begins 6/1/93. Entries must be received by 12/30/94. Not responsible for lost, late, damaged, misdirected, illegible or postage due mail. Mechanically reproduced entries are not eligible. All entries become property of the sponsor and will not be returned.

Prize Selection/Validations: Selection of winners will be conducted no later than 5:00 PM on January 28, 1995, by an independent judging organization whose decisions are final. Random drawings will be held at 1211 Avenue of the Americas, New York, N.Y. 10036. Entrants need not be present to win. Odds of winning are determined by total number of entries received. Circulation of this sweepstakes is estimated not to exceed 200 million. All prizes are guaranteed to be awarded and delivered to winners. Winners will be notified by mail and may be required to complete an affidavit of eligibility and release of liability which must be returned within 14 days of date on notification or alternate winners will be selected in a random drawing. Any prize notification letter or any prize returned to a participating sponsor, Bantam Doubleday Dell Publishing Group, Inc., its participating divisions or subsidiaries, or the independent judging organization as undeliverable will be awarded to an alternate winner. Prizes are not transferable. No substitution for prizes except as offered or as may be necessary due to unavailability, in which case a prize of equal or greater value will be awarded. Prizes will be awarded approximately 90 days after the drawing. All taxes are the sole responsibility of the winners. Entry constitutes permission (except where prohibited by law) to use winners' names, hometowns, and likenesses for publicity purposes without further or other compensation. Prizes won by minors will be awarded in the name of parent or legal guardian.

Participation: Sweepstakes open to residents of the United States and Canada except for the province of Quebec. Sweepstakes sponsored by Bantam Doubleday Dell Publishing Group, Inc., (BDD), 1540 Broadway, New York, NY 10036. Versions of this sweepstakes with different graphics and prize choices will be offered in conjunction with various solicitations or promotions by different subsidiaries and divisions of BDD. Where applicable, winners will have their choice of any prize offered at level won. Employees of BDD, its divisions, subsidiaries, advertising agencies, independent judging organization, and their immediate family members are not eligible.

Canadian residents, in order to win, must first correctly answer a time limited arithmetical skill testing question. Void in Puerto Rico, Quebec and wherever prohibited or restricted by law. Subject to all federal, state, local and provincial laws and regulations. For a list of major prize winners (available after 1/29/95): send a self addressed, stamped envelope entirely separate from your entry to: Sweepstakes Winners, P.O. Box 517, Gibbstown, NJ 08027. Requests must be received by 12/30/94. DO NOT SEND ANY OTHER CORRESPONDENCE TO THIS P.O. BOX.